Ring of Desire

Ring of Desire

Ryshia Kennie

Black Lyon Publishing, LLC

RING OF DESIRE
Copyright © 2009 by RYSHIA KENNIE

Our books may be ordered through your local bookstore or by visiting the publisher:

www.BlackLyonPublishing.com

Black Lyon Publishing, LLC
PO Box 567
Baker City, OR 97814

This is a work of fiction. All of the characters, names, events, organizations and conversations in this novel are either the products of the author's vivid imagination or are used in a fictitious way for the purposes of this story.

ISBN-10:   1-934912-20-4
ISBN-13:   978-1-934912-20-1
Library of Congress Control Number: 2009934528

Written, published and printed in
the United States of America.

Black Lyon Paranormal Romance

For Linda—some people you can always count on.

Chapter One

Southern England 1072

I will not die.

Vala turned her head blindly toward the shore. She spat a stream of water and choked as the chair lurched and her neck snapped forward. Her head spun as she twisted in circles over the water. Her wrists ached and burned as the wet rope cut into them.

"Again!" the priest commanded.

The rope played through the smith's reluctant hands. The chair began to lower.

"Nay," she whispered and grimaced at the pain in her throat that was raw from swallowing water and the silent screams of those she defended.

Her bare toes touched the unusual chill that sheeted the river. Water closed over her head. The water wrapped around her like a cold, silken blanket. Her nostrils quivered and her throat ached from holding her breath.

How much longer?

Vala wrapped her fingers around the rough rope. The elements she could touch—rope, water, chair—were fast becoming her only reality, her only link to the physical world.

When she thought she could take no more, the chair began to move upward. Her lungs ached and rivets of pain clawed her chest. She thought she would die if she did not get air. She gasped as her head broke the surface.

"Ye will obey." The priest's words were spewed in sharp hate-edged pellets.

"Let her go." A woman's voice broke the silence.

"Aye," another agreed.

"She's had enough." This time the women seemed to speak as one.

Vala's teeth chattered as the chill spring wind wrapped around her wet body. She thought of Rosaline, with her stillborn son at her side, alone and dying because of a Norman. She sucked in a breath as heat flooded her body. With a gasp she twisted the chair so she faced the shore.

You are the chosen. It is not time. The voices of the Ancients rippled deep within her soul. Everything is, as it was foretold.

"Cease!" a man roared.

"'Tis I who give orders!" Alfred, who had presented himself as a priest not so many months ago, puffed his flabby chest, adjusted the rope around his waist and glared out at Vala.

"I will not," she persisted through the chafe and rawness of her throat. "It will kill her."

"Stubborn wretch. Again!" the priest demanded.

The priest swung a hand in the direction of the smith whose expression was agonized as he clutched the rope that controlled the chair.

"It will be done." Alfred motioned again for the rope to be lowered.

Vala pulled in a deep mouthful of air. She waited. Nothing. Cynn, the blacksmith, hadn't moved. He clutched the rope that still held the chair clear of the water.

"Nay." The sound broke almost before it escaped Vala's lips.

"Nay? How dare you, witch. Ye will not refuse me. Ye will admit your wrong and right it."

"No wrong." Vala could barely get the words out and against everything that Magna had taught her she threw her aura in the priest's path. To the Ancients, an aura was a powerful thing. It could take down a man. But it was a weak effort and only the gold cross on his thick chest glinted sparks in the dull mist.

Destiny, girl, you do not have the power to change.

Hope swelled through her at the sound of Magna's voice. Magna, she had always been here a part of Hafne even in the time before Vala could remember.

You can give it to me, she threw the thought out.

But Magna was silent and in the silence Vala knew. There would be no magic that would rescue her this day.

"No wrong!" Alfred almost screeched the words. "You are a woman, unclean from birth. You are nothing. Men have the power and you would be wise to remember that." His voice became softer. "Even here."

Feminine gasps followed this statement, for it was not the way of Hafne.

"Dunk her, dunk her!" The priest screamed.

Words of a chant that no priest would ever utter confirmed everything that Vala already knew. Alfred was no real priest. He was one of the Others.

The words seemed to come from everywhere and from nowhere.

Fires of hell ... fires of hell ... hell ... hell ...

•

Home.

The sun sparked weakly through the fog-shrouded trees. The dirt and grime of many campaigns were forgotten. This was his reward, his own keep.

Finally, after all these years of soldiering for William he would have his land, a home, people who were his to defend. He urged the horse faster. Ramion complied readily with powerful legs that lengthened and hugged the earth with long strides.

"Anxious?" Royce urged his steed to keep pace.

Giles grinned back at his friend. "Aye."

They slowed as the clearing closed again to solid oak trees. He glanced behind him where the glint of mail reflected through the trees and his entourage of thirty men trailed them.

"A keep teaming with servants, a village fifty strong, that is something to look forward to. You're a lucky man, Giles."

"Not luck," Giles answered and thought of the years fighting uprisings on the continent. Hard years and he had given his youth to the cause.

"You are right. We were only boys when we first saw battle." Royce chuckled and pulled his splayed fingers through hair that was newly streaked with gray. "Now look at us."

"Tis hard to believe that we have sat these saddles for ten years."

"Some days not so hard," Royce said. "Tis glad I'll be to settle into this keep of yours. I may not move for many days."

Giles slowed the horse's pace and settled into the saddle. "With this weather I doubt anyone will want to leave shelter. The rain has not let up since we entered these lands."

"Maybe that is a good sign. Rich land, many rains," Royce answered.

Giles glanced around and saw the rich loamy carpet on the forest floor, heard the chatter of a squirrel and the chirp of birds and knew that Royce spoke true. The forest rustled as a deer burst through the dense bush and bounded in delicate leaps across their path.

A soft hum came from nowhere and Giles' hand tightened on the pommel. He listened with a warrior's ability to hear the slightest nuance. He heard it again, a sound alien to the whisper and rustle of the forest ... voices.

"Do ye hear that?" He glanced at Royce.

Royce leaned forward. "I hear nothing."

The trees thinned. A faint movement, a flash of color flitted through the trees.

"Stay back." Giles commanded as he dropped the reins. He leapt from his horse and edged closer. He could hear voices, a low distant murmur. Branches obscured his vision. Then he saw them. At the edge of a river a group of people were gathered around a priest. It was only a baptism or some similar religious rite.

Giles' gaze pulled beyond the riverbank to the first sight of his holding. A ragtag group of weathered huts clustered just back from the river. The rough settlement bowed beneath the shadow of two imposing towers that pierced the low hugging clouds and imprinted their presence in the grey sky. He sucked in a shaky breath.

"Jesu!" he muttered. This was all his. "Unbelievable."

Movement caught and pulled his gaze once again to the river. A limp figure lifted and bobbed in the current.

"By the Saint's Holy Bones!"

This was no baptism.

He moved quickly and silently to reach his horse. In one fluid movement he leapt on the horse and took the reins.

"What—" Royce began but was silenced by the look Giles shot him. Royce nodded his head in the silent communication they had developed through years of battle together.

Giles waved his arm, the signal for his men to move out. He pushed the horse into a gallop.

Excitement surged through Giles as he urged his horse forward. A battle, small skirmish, it did not matter, he loved it all. Behind him the sound of the horses meshed as they pounded the earth in a determined rumble and matched the thump of blood roaring in his veins. A woman clutched her child tight to her side, another screamed. It was a brief sound that cut off abruptly as he and his men broke through the low shrub of the forest edge.

They were a ragged, filthy group that flanked the riverbank and they turned their backs to him. They dared to ignore him!

Anger drove him forward, into the crowd. They would know who was lord. People scattered, running in all directions to avoid the flying hooves. Giles raised his hand, signaling his men to wait for his next command.

"*Arête!*" he roared. "Halt!"

"Normans," someone whispered.

The man in a cassock with a cross dangling on his thick chest, obviously a priest, turned his attention back to the chair held by a wooden beam and angled across the river. The figure that hung beneath the beam was slumped forward and unmoving.

"Lower it now!" the priest screeched.

"*Mon Dieu! Parlez pas!*" Giles stopped. He had slipped into his mother tongue. A language these Saxons would not understand. He must speak English. He drew in a breath and roared, "Silence! What has the creature done?"

"This punishment is not for man to question," the priest shot back. "Lower the chair."

A harsh collective breath rasped through the crowd as the chair dropped.

Giles moved his steed forward to the edge of the crowd. "Punishment for what?"

Silence breathed around him.

"Who ere you?" The priest demanded.

"I am Lord de Montford. King William has given me this keep, these lands and its people. You answer to me. Who are you?" Cold weariness warred with his anger.

"Alfred, I am their priest and their salvation!"

Giles' gaze swung to the huge man who strained to hold the

rope that controlled the beam and ultimately the chair that dangled over the river. The man's face was pale and his hands shook. With a nod to Giles he rammed an elbow into Alfred's side. The priest grunted as he landed on his backside.

"My lord." The big man's deep voice trembled and his massive upper arms quivered.

The rope slipped.

Giles leapt from his horse and pushed through the crowd.

"Who does he think he is?" A woman asked.

"Bloody King mayhap," another said.

"Quiet!" another woman interjected. "Stop the priest!"

"Aye! Save Vala." A chorus of women's voices sounded from all sides.

The rope picked up speed and with a heavy splash dropped the chair into the river. Giles grabbed the rope as the last lengths of hemp played out. He dug his heels in and leaned back adding leverage to muscle. Suddenly the tension eased and it became easy. Royce was at his back.

Chanting began. Instinctively Giles knew that it was not of the Church. Not the Church that he knew.

Giles' lips tightened as the chair broke water and swung free. The figure didn't move. Were it not for the ropes, it would have fallen into the water. Beneath the beam the chair pitched wildly before the two men were able to ease it to shore.

The chair dropped to the ground with a thud and fell forward. Giles pulled his dagger and dragged it quickly through the rope that held the body.

"A woman," Royce muttered.

"A woman, are you sure?"

"Tits," Royce muttered.

They both leaned forward.

Giles raised her chin. "You're right." He released her and swiveled to look behind at the silent crowd that gaped at him.

A small sound made him look behind. The girl lay on her side, sprawled in a rapidly pooling puddle of muddy water.

"She is dead," Royce said.

Giles nudged the pathetic creature hoping for a spark of life. A burial and a trial! The tasks were compounding and he had not even gained entrance to the keep.

It was then that the body chose to cough. For a minute, a harsh gasp was the only sound on that over crowded riverbank. Then she spewed over the boots of both knights.

"Jesu!" Giles roared as both he and Royce jumped back.

She groaned and tried to roll over.

Giles moved forward and gently lifted her. The girl's eyes opened. Her eyes were so blue, so filled with emotion that he almost dropped her. She closed her eyes.

Giles swung around to face the crowd of villagers. His villagers. He swallowed heavily. "Has the girl any relatives amongst you?

Only the harsh breaths of the winded smith and the soft jangle of the warhorses broke the stillness.

"She belongs with me, my lord."

The woman must have been at the back of the crowd for she seemed to come from nowhere. Giles frowned. Not "she is my relative," but "she belongs with me."

"Your name."

"Magna, my lord." She peered up at him from a face framed in wisps of gray hair. A face that was unlined, smooth like a child's.

The girl shifted in his arms and moaned.

"You will be blessed." The old woman's eyes grazed every inch of him.

Eyes too old in a face too young. The thought popped into his head even as his eyes locked involuntarily with the woman's.

What manner of being was this? He had no belief in the fairies of the woods yet this woman …

"Show me your hut." He turned even as he said it and strode toward the village. He knew the woman would have to run. He wanted that—anything to regain control for she had set him decidedly off edge.

"There, my lord," she puffed as she pointed at the little hovel.

Giles turned to face the crowd, his people, and the stench was overwhelming as they followed. His men flanked the rear herding any strays like misguided sheep.

"All of you will have your say in this matter before the morrow's nooning meal. When your fast is broken be at the hall."

If there was a hall, he thought, and shifted his slight burden. He was assuming much of a holding yet unknown.

"A trial, my lord?" Alfred squeaked and his jowls swayed.

"I will say nothing more on the matter til tomorrow."

"A trial," a large boned woman said and crossed herself.

"Drown us." A stringy haired blonde woman scurried away from him dragging a child with her.

"Hang us," a young woman with greasy hair restrained in a braid suggested.

"The dungeon," another young woman guessed.

Giles blocked the rest of the comments out. They would learn soon enough what his intentions were.

The girl stirred as he shouldered the rough wooden door open. It swung easily, the gapped rough wood offering little protection from either the weather or marauders.

The old woman scurried past him. Giles followed her and laid the girl in the corner on a straw mat that smelled surprisingly fresh. A fire danced in the corner, its bright light cheering the grim little room. A strand of hair, caked with mud, hung across the girl's face. He brushed it back and saw the glint in the firelight. Even filthy, it was blonde. Saxon hair.

He drew back to wipe his hand on the side of his tunic and stopped. His tunic was warm. Concealed in the leather pouch beneath his tunic, the seer's stone vibrated gently. He dragged his hand across his tunic again but now the cloth was cool. Mayhap it had been his imagination. Yet the room was alive with whispers, faint sounds that seemed to come from the very walls. He wiped his hand again.

"Won't do any good." The old woman's voice echoed eerily behind him, the sound seeming to come from everywhere and nowhere. She cackled. "Tainted ye are, by a Saxon."

His eyes narrowed. Human, maybe, but she appeared more creature than woman. Wizened face, wild gray hair, full youthful lips, it was all a sharp contrast to the wrinkled folds of skin on her neck. The hands, like the lips, were flush with youth. He couldn't remove his eyes from her. It was as if he were under a spell. It was as if she looked to his soul. Impossible!

"Is there a healer in the village?" he asked, trying to ignore her cryptic words. The strange connection he had with the creature was only a trick of the shadows and light dancing in the hut. She was nothing more than an old crone, a hag.

He waited. The old woman did not move. The girl groaned on

her straw pallet.

"If there is anything you need. Herbs, clothes, come to me at the keep. I'll see ye get what ye need."

The old woman muttered unintelligible words over the girl. It could only be the shadows that cloaked this place. It could be nothing else. Yet in a blink, the taut, unmarred hands that had worked over the girl were now the mottled, frail hands of the very old.

He shrugged. There was nothing he could do here. He ducked his head as he emerged from the hut and blinked for even the faint light from the mist-shrouded day seemed bright.

From deep within the hovel he thought he heard words. He must be over exhausted. But still, those words wove through his mind.

He is the One ... the One ... the One.

Chapter Two

With the strange fey words still echoing in his head, Giles pulled himself onto Ramion's back. He raised his arm in the air and motioned his men forward. Ahead, the towers cut deep silhouettes against the murky sky.

Within the hidden pouch the seer's stone hummed. This time the warning was not his imagination.

Alfred was no man of the cloth, and yet the villagers listened. Why? Giles thumbed the stone and vowed he would soon find the truth. For a minute, blue eyes filled his mind and he had an overwhelming desire to go back, to see her, to touch her and to make sure that she was real. The girl he had rescued felt like she was branded in his mind as easily as the soft feel of her had imprinted on his body. "Ridiculous," he muttered.

Giles forced his attention on the job at hand. He judged the keep a mere quarter mile from the village but the distance stretched onward. The horses' hooves echoed behind him and the keep seemed to come no nearer. As they broke the cover of the ancient oaks, silence met them. From the village to the keep there had been no sounds to mute the heavy tread of the war horses. Not even the trill of a bird's song marred the stillness.

The late afternoon sun streaked dimly through the fog. Giles wiped his sleeve across his face and his gaze swept the broken wood of the palisade.

"It is doubtful it will withstand any sort of attack. It is wood and in bad shape." Royce's voice was almost apologetic.

She was naught but a girl but yet she was not—she was a woman. And she had fit so sweetly against him. Giles looked over his shoulder as if expecting the girl they had rescued to be there.

"Giles, are you listening?"

"Aye." He frowned at Royce. His saddle shifted beneath him as he moved the reins to his right hand and stroked the cold sweat that matted his destrier's proud neck. "You expected more of a Saxon keep?"

"Appears like any other, yet ..."

"Yet?"

"But for the many breaches."

"By the Saints, Royce, the outer walls are falling down. I thought Wulfgar was gone long before the invasion but the walls are marked as if they have seen fierce combat."

She had been so fragile and delicate in his arms. He forced his attention back to his keep. His own keep, it was his dream since boyhood.

"I doubt there's enough stone that we can reach without struggle. The cliffs look as if they drop straight to the sea." Royce frowned.

"There is much stone and within easy reach." Giles motioned toward the coast where water drove against the sharp cliffs. The stone warmed and in his mind, Giles' saw what lay behind the keep. "There is a path."

A brisk wind skittered around them. From the depths of the forest, chill air spread fingers of fog along the ground. The heavy fog settled beneath the weathered wood of the palisade and disappeared from sight.

Would she be cold this night? "Jesu!" He spat as if that curse would drive the thoughts of the girl from his mind. What sort of place was this that he couldn't stop thinking of her?

"Did you feel that?" Royce asked.

"Nothing more than a breeze," Giles said and willed himself to believe it.

The gate hung crookedly. There were gaps in the wood and the iron hinges were mostly broken. The courtyard was covered with cobbles that were raised and broken, and slick with moss. Dank rot scented the air that, and something else. It was faint, yet pungent and it hung over the courtyard.

Giles swung in the saddle to view his men close behind him. A cloud of dust swirled around them.

Dust, he thought. Despite the obvious damp and recent rain

there was dust.

Giles dismounted.

"Gilroy, find water." He gestured to one of his men. Gilroy's tasks were always small. He'd been addled since being struck by a mace two battles ago.

Giles threw Ramion's reins to Robert who he charged with the horses. "The rest of you, get the tents set up. We'll use them for the next few days until we have seen what awaits us inside."

"My lord, I do not like this place," Ainsley ventured.

Giles glanced at the boy who looked down quickly to hide his blush. "It is an uneasy place but maybe it is just because no one has lived here for so long." He chucked the boy lightly under the chin. "Have I trained you such? Like a mewling babe?"

The boy shook his head and straightened his shoulders.

"I thought not. Come."

With the boy tagging his heels and Royce at his side, Giles strode toward the first building in the bailey.

The solid little building was obviously empty and long unused. The door swung in the soft breeze. The breeze was all that was left of the chill fog that had swept in only minutes before. Rusted hinges screeched.

The smell of rotted, burned wood hit him as soon as Giles cleared the doorway. Overhead the roof was seared in odd spots and blackened as if someone had held a torch here and there. In the middle of the empty room, a pot hung over the silent fire pit. Iron chains holding the pot began to creak as the pot moved slowly back and forth.

"My lord," Ainsley began in a voice that was choked and an octave higher than normal.

Giles bent over the pot. It was rimmed with black, hardened chunks of what might have once been food. He picked up a bowl from a small wooden table. A pestle stuck to the inside.

"Tis as if they left in a great hurry," Royce said.

"Possibly," Giles responded. "Left while the meal was still cooking. Why?"

"Invasion?"

"Nay, that is six years past." Giles rubbed his chin. "This keep was not part of the first invasion nor any of the one's that followed. It has been without an overlord for years and thus surrendered peacefully. Wulfgar was gone before the invasion even began."

He frowned. Everything about this place spoke of flight, of fright, and of a people on the run.

"Whatever happened is long done. We'll probably never know," Giles said with a voice coached in optimism for the boy's sake. "Shall we see to the keep?"

"It looks solid enough," Royce ventured as they approached.

"Jesu!" Giles breathed.

They stood in front of the large doors barred by a log strapped across the entrance. A cart heaped with stone was rammed sideways against the wooden doors.

"Barred from the outside." Royce scratched his massive forehead. "Something inside can't get out," he muttered and stepped backward, stumbling on a loose cobble.

"I found water." Gilroy appeared, out of breath and with his usual lack of finesse. "They barred the door?" His brows shot up as he took in the cart. "From the outside?"

"Aye," Giles replied shortly. "You found water? A well?"

"Around the corner. Water's good. No smell. Had some myself." His smile only revealed a mouthful of broken, blackened teeth.

"Good, tell Robert. He can see the horses are watered. Ainsley, help him." He guided the boy with a light push on his shoulder.

"Aye, my lord."

Giles turned back to the massive oak doors and thumped his fist against it. The sound was dull, heavy and ended abruptly.

"No echo," Royce said. "Tis beyond normal."

"You have heard too many stories."

"Mayhap."

"It stands strong." Giles placed a hand on the door. "Yet the villagers are no where near and the place looks deserted. I fear the answers are inside."

Together they lifted rocks from the cart and piled them aside. The rocks were large and uncommonly difficult to lift.

Sweat dripped and stung his eyes as Giles dragged the back of his hand across his brow. They pushed with everything they had and the cart only rocked. Suddenly the cart began to roll easily forward. Giles peered over the top to see the huge back of the smith, with the tongue of the vehicle across his back and his muscles straining against his threadbare tunic. Within seconds the cart was away from the entrance.

"Not wise," the big man muttered as he rubbed his hands against his filthy tunic. "There for a reason."

The smith refused to meet Giles' eyes.

"What reason?" Giles demanded.

"To keep the demons in."

"Demons?"

"Aye."

"The unholy, the undead. Those without blessing of Church." A new voice interjected.

The smith was swept aside as Alfred, the priest, elbowed him out of the way.

"Gentle as a lamb and just as bright," Alfred snorted as the smith hurried out of the bailey. "Like I said the unholy, undead. That is what lies behind that door." He smiled. "That and a ghost or two but that is of no consequence."

"Who blocked the door?" Giles demanded. It seemed like he had been demanding since his arrival. He liked it not.

"The smith was right. Although I prefer that you have opened the keep and that you do not close it again." Dark eyes that reflected nothing met Giles. "You will not close it again. Your curiosity will not allow otherwise. Will it?" The look he gave Giles was almost taunting.

"You dare to speak such to me." Giles strode toward him.

"Nay, you will not throttle me."

Giles started. The man had read his thoughts.

"I know much." The priest backed up. "Even your very thoughts," he said as he lifted his robe and jogged toward the relative safety of the village.

"Do you think there was some truth in what he said?" Royce spat and crossed himself.

"I do not know. I do know that I will find out before the next moon turns."

"You've dreamt again."

Giles shrugged and turned his attention to the door.

When the great doors finally swung open the stench of burnt wood met them. The floor rustled as small animals scurried to escape through the rotted rushes. Giles fought the urge to turn and leave this dank place. He felt the evil deep within his soul. It whispered to him. Ominous vibrations fluttered within the leather pouch beneath his tunic. Instinctively, he pressed an index finger to his forehead in an attempt to silence the sound.

"I hope this is not England's best," Royce joked but his voice shimmered with unease.

"Not now, but it will be." Giles forced himself to the present and punched his friend lightly in the arm.

"You are serious?"

Giles strode forward. He heard Royce's footsteps behind him. A scent of lavender drifted lightly around him and he thought of her, of the girl. "Enough," he muttered and shook his head.

"What do you think?" Royce asked.

"I don't know. But whatever happened here, it wasn't good. The villagers are frightened. They obviously haven't come near this place in a long time." Giles' gaze shifted to the cobwebs that slanted across the stairs leading to the next level. "No one has."

"Superstitious lot. Most things frighten them."

"True." Giles shrugged his shoulders. But for a moment his thoughts drifted to her, the one he had rescued. The thought that she might have been frightened disturbed him and he didn't know why. He tested a beam and found it sturdy. Only here and there were the beams charred. "Looks like the cooking hut. Controlled fire, watched, purposeful." He glanced over his shoulder. "Don't you agree?"

"Or intense and focused on one spot."

"Possibly."

The room was large and empty except for the massive chair that still remained on the dais and the trestle tables that stood in the hall. Giles leaned on a table. It moved as a leg wobbled. He lifted his hand. "Let us hope there is a woodworker in the village."

The second floor was empty. The wooden floor broken in places but there was no sign of the charring that had been downstairs. They ventured across the wooden planks that creaked and groaned under their weight. Below, they could see the hall clearly where whole planks had been removed. Gingerly they skirted the gaps in the floor.

"God's teeth!" Royce hissed as he slipped on a loose plank and his boot punched air.

"Watch yourself." Giles said automatically. They entered a

corridor and the gloaming spread over everything, the darkness collecting in the corners and stretching across the floor. "Should have brought a candle," he muttered and tripped on a loose board. Shrill squeaking followed his words, high pitched and as quickly, gone.

"Rats." Royce roared. "Is there anything worse?"

"We shall soon see," Giles replied calmly as he came to the end of the hall to a heavy oak door. With a light push the door swung easily open.

Royce shouldered in beside him. "A bed platform! I can't believe this. What manner of Saxon are they?"

"No Saxon that we have ever seen," Giles replied and stepped into the room. The Saxon holdings were primitive. Despite the fact that the bed platform was the only furnishing, there was nothing primitive about this holding. Cobwebs hung in a grey mesh over the bed and from the rafters tendrils drifted through the air.

Giles sneezed and backed out. "There is much here. I did not expect this of a Saxon holding."

Giles walked back to the stairs. "It is a great mystery, a Saxon keep with a second floor, with stairs."

Their stiff leather boots thudded softly as they went down the steps. On the main floor the walls were built five feet up with stone before the wood timbers began. On the wood portion, patches of the wall appeared lighter. Banners had once decorated these walls. *No*, he thought, *not possible.*

"Could it be Roman leavings?" Royce suggested.

"It was built by others, not Saxons or Romans." Giles did not explain the knowledge but it was a surety. He could feel it like others might read letters on a manuscript.

Giles skimmed a finger over the stone. A keep partially built in stone, with stairs leading to an upper floor and with a definite feeling of a presence. Trust his luck - he'd been gifted with a problem.

Warm breath fanned his neck. He jerked around, pulling his sword at the same time. There was no one, only the stairs and beyond that the darkness of the endless cavernous space. Still, he held his breath and listened.

Many years have we waited.

It was one voice, yet it was many and seemed to have no fixed origin. Royce was trolling the edges of the hall and had obviously heard nothing.

Many years have you been foretold.

This time it was only one voice and it seemed to come from directly behind him. He swung yet again and his sword cut air.

That got Royce's attention. Beside him in seconds, Royce stood with sword outstretched.

"You heard it too?"

"Heard? Nay but…"

"Silence!" Giles roared not sure if he meant Royce or the unknown voice.

The chuckle for all its softness was strident, demanding.

You trust too much in the ways of man.

The scent of onions assailed him and then the creature, the old woman, the hag, whatever she was, stood before him.

"What is your name?" he commanded.

"Who goes there?" Royce asked and jostled Giles, as he thrust his sword before him.

Startled, Giles turned to him. "Do you see her?"

"See? There is nothing there."

And there wasn't. Where the hag had stood there was now nothing, only air. But the air was not silent.

Magna. Do you remember me?

And he did. Somewhere deep in his memory he remembered not the hag of the village who had claimed the girl but a woman of a long time ago. But the memory was faint and quickly slipped away.

He turned his attention immediately back to Royce. This mystery was his alone and he would solve it. In the meantime, he would not be acting the whimsical fool.

"Let's go," he commanded.

They stepped out into the courtyard. Some of the tents were up but the horses were still milling in the yard.

"Robert," Giles called to the man who appeared from amid the milling horses, holding a sack of oats in one hand. "Where did you find that? Show me." As they rounded the corner of the keep he noticed the dried branches of a creeping plant clung halfway up the side of the wall. He made a note to have it torn down. The plant would only mean easy access to any enemy that made it past the palisade.

"You think there's a stable here?" Robert asked.

"Seems likely." Giles did not add his own doubts. "Is that the hut?" he asked and pushed open the door. Inside, it was sturdy but small and in a corner there were four more sacks of oats.

Giles fingered the bag that hung inside his tunic. The pouch vibrated and strummed. He removed his hand and dropped it to his side. Still the stone would not be silenced. He shuddered and forced his thoughts away from the seer's stone as the rumble of his men's voices in the distance brought him back to the present.

A whicker broke above the distant sound of the low voices of his men and the low throaty voice of a stallion responded. Ramion. He'd recognize his call anywhere. Ramion trumpeted again, a stallion's call to a mare. But there were no mares here. The villagers had no horses that Giles knew of. There were only the horses of his men and none were mares.

Giles stepped out of the hut. He rounded the far corner of the keep and there it stood. A long building, its wood darkened with age.

The stable's doors hung broken and partially open. He pushed at the doors and for an instant nothing happened. Then in a rush they gave. Giles fumbled to regain his footing as he was thrown inside. He blinked in the faint light. It was a solid little building. Fresh straw littered the floor, and in the shadows he saw a glossy head and intelligent eyes watching him.

"God's teeth," he muttered and hurried forward. The animal swung her chocolate gaze toward him and nudged her nose over the rail of her stall. He stroked her velvety nose with gentle fingers. Her chestnut coat gleamed in the soft light. "What are you doing here, beauty?"

Giles reached into the pouch at his waist. His hand closed around the stone that had always rung true. Since he was a small boy he had relied on its warnings. The stone was the only thing that linked him to his distant and mostly unknown heritage. The only thing good wrought from his mother. Despite all that, for the first time he felt no comfort from the warmth the seer's stone emitted.

Chapter Three

That night Giles dreamt of her, of the one he had rescued yesterday. She held his hand and whispered in his ear like he had known her forever. Yet he had only held her briefly when he had carried her, wet and cold, to her hut.

"I have loved you always," she whispered and around them shadows danced.

"We were destined to be together." He nuzzled her neck and gathered her soft curves closer to him. And nearby, birds the size of small children shrieked from their perches in trees brilliant and unearthly lime green. He smoothed her hair, silken and richly thick and so exotically free of cover. It had taken him so long to find her. He would never let her go.

"You believe." She wrapped her arms around his neck.

"This place is magical," he agreed. "As are you." He picked her up, meaning to take her home and to keep her near him forever. For in the depths of his dream he knew she was meant only for him.

"My name is Vala," she said before she slipped from his arms and dropped lightly to the ground.

"Lord Giles!" The voice was male and no part of this scene.

He blinked heavily and stared into his squire's face. "Ainsley?" He rubbed sleep grit from his eyes but the dream hung in thick cobwebs around him and it took him a minute to separate the dream from the reality.

"You dreamt, my lord?"

"Aye."

"You spoke of love." The boy giggled.

"Be gone," Giles ordered as he stood up and stretched before pushing the tent flap aside and striding outside. Today he would begin setting this place to rights. And then, then he would find her, Vala. He frowned. T'was a dream, odds were that was not her name. Yet in his gut, he knew that was not true. She was Vala and one day she would be his.

"Jesu! De Montford," he quietly chastised himself. He took a deep breath and as he had his entire life, forced himself back to reality.

•

That day the hall was ripe with the scent of sour bodies. Giles tried to breathe as little of the rank air as possible. The foul odor that filled the hall could have easily ended any war.

The sound of retching pulled his attention from the villagers. His squire ran from the hall, his hand covering his mouth.

A short woman with hair in a long stringy braid that escaped her wimple sneered at him and spat on the floor.

"Cease that," Giles said evenly.

She spat again.

"Who are you?"

"Cecile."

"That is a Norman name. Yet you are Saxon."

"Filthy Norman!" The woman drew her words out slowly then pursed her lips and spat again.

"Remove her." He stood up.

A rumble of voices built in the hall. The villagers crowded together.

"Nay, my lord," Cecile pleaded. "Nay, not that. Do not have them sport with me."

"Sport with you!" Giles almost laughed at the thought. The woman was filthy and her lips sunk over gums that held few teeth. Her pinched, ugly face would not have been attractive even in the first blush of her youth. "My men do not sport with the likes of you."

Giles motioned for Robert, who lifted the Saxon hag over his shoulder and carried her screaming from the keep.

"Does anyone else wish to defy me?" He said the words softly into the silent room. Feet shuffled but no one spoke. He sat down. He'd gained their attention. His gaze scanned the room. She wasn't here. The girl he had rescued was not among them.

"The one you tortured, she lives?"

"I do not know." The priest's bare feet curled on the dirt floor.

"You do not know. Alfred, how is that possible?" Giles blinked the grit from his eyes. He had had a poor night's sleep. He should have gone back to the hut and seen if the girl they tortured had lived or died.

She must live! Where had that thought come from? Giles reached for his eating dagger. His finger smoothed over the blade. He tried to ignore the strange cold that raised the hairs on his arm when his gaze caught Alfred's.

"It would not matter my lord, if she lived or died." Alfred's eyes were black and unfathomable.

"False!" shrieked a large woman.

Giles' attention returned Alfred. "Why did you torture her?"

"The witch helped birth a babe."

"Helped at a birthing? Woman's work."

Alfred's face reddened and angry veins began to throb in his neck. "Evil."

"Evil?" Giles' nostrils quivered as the scent of decay briefly swept the air.

"Women, they are simple creatures easy to possess for demons and such. Women must be helped and guided if they are not to be thrown to the heat of hell. After birthing, the cleansing must be done before anything else and that one…" Alfred whispered.

"The one you were torturing?"

"She used water, plain water, unholy water."

Giles thumbed his dagger. Birthing – women's work. He had a keep in bad shape and much work to be done.

Alfred began to shriek. "Hell, fires of hell. Damned…"

"Enough!" Giles held a hand up.

"The woman that give birth, she has a name?" Giles turned to the silent group of villagers.

"Rosaline," said the same tall, raw-boned woman who had spoken earlier. She wiped away a tear. "Her name was Rosaline."

"And your name?"

"Editha."

Giles turned his attention back to Alfred.

"She needed to be cleansed," Alfred repeated.

"How?" His thumbnail tapped lightly against the broken arm of the dais chair. He would have to get the woodworker tomorrow. He shifted his thoughts back to the priest.

"Dirt." The priest's voice was soft but echoed in the stillness. "God's own dirt."

"Dirt!" Giles bellowed and leapt to his feet.

"An uncommon practice, my lord." The voice was mellow and sure, and a woman's.

Giles turned to see the hag standing beside him. How had she gotten there?

He glanced to Royce whose attention was on the priest. Giles stroked his chin. Was it possible that Royce did not see the hag?

"Who are you?" he whispered under his breath.

"You know me by many names. They know me as Magna."

Giles glanced up and caught Royce's puzzled expression.

"An uncommon practice, my lord, to pack the birthing canal with dirt. Part of the dark art they practice to weaken the power of women."

"Cleanse it … art?" Giles roared. "What nonsense do you speak? Where is the woman who gave birth? Bring her to me!" The echoes of his command splintered off the rough walls and bounced across the stricken faces.

"Of what do you speak," Royce whispered urgently. "You confuse." He frowned. "Are you not well?"

"I …" Giles frowned. "You do not hear nor see."

"She was cursed from the beginning." Magna ran a finger along the arm of his chair. "Women hold the truth of much in this land. For this is a land like no other."

Magna's image faded in and out. Glimpses of a beautiful nubile woman and then a leathered wrinkled old crone. The two images seemed to blend and overlay one on top of the other. He rubbed a hand across his eyes hoping to clear his vision. It did not change.

She winked at him.

The priest and the others strengthen the curse.

"What is this talk about a curse?" Giles asked to no one in particular.

There was a gasp in the otherwise silent room.

"de Montford," Turstin, one of his warriors, whispered urgently. "Do you see the hag?"

"You too?" Giles asked. "Jesu! This is uncommonly strange. You saw her …"

"Disappear," Turstin leaned closer. "The others …" He nodded to Giles' men. "They do not see. Not yet."

"What do you mean, not yet?"

"I don't know." Turstin shrugged. "But since we arrived here, I know things that mayhap I should not."

"Enough talk." Giles waved him back. "She is only a fey old woman."

"And the others have bad eyesight?" Turstin smiled crookedly.

"If you wish."

"What are you whispering about?" Royce broke in.

"Nothing of import," Giles said roughly. He took his attention back to the villagers. "The woman that gave birth. Bring her to me immediately."

"She is dead." The voice was firm and unafraid. Magna. He did not turn around. Fairy or not she was definitely not of this earth.

The One.

Had he imagined the words?

"What is it, my lord?" Magna was back as if she had never disappeared.

He shifted uncomfortably. "Nothing."

The faintest smile graced Magna's full lips.

Giles turned his attention to the priest. "You continued after I told you cease? I commanded you cease."

"Cease only the water torture. You said nothing about the other." The priest puffed his chest and hitched the rope around his bulging middle. "I am of the Church. I would not touch one such as she." He smirked. "I did not have to. Death wanted her. So, my lord," he drawled the words. "I obeyed. Beelzebub took her."

"Leave! Leave immediately!" Giles' voice broke a notch lower and he only wanted to leap forward and kill the man.

Alfred smiled crookedly up at him. "I'll return when you are in a better humor perhaps."

"This keep. The village."

"The keep? The village?" The smile slipped.

"Both!" Giles roared and nodded to Royce.

Everyone began to talk at once and the villagers' voices merged together.

"The priest … never before."

"Because they can't. Unless they have ..."

"... the magic." A smaller, thin woman finished. "You don't suppose?"

Editha's voice rang out as she addressed the room at large. "Cease this talk of priest. The man was no more priest than I." She glanced around. "He only wants the Rogue to live and for that he must control the women; control Vala." She paused. "He was no priest," she muttered as the whispers built around her.

"You will regret this." Alfred's voice was high pitched as he was dragged toward the door. "This land is his! You will die! You will see. You will die, my lord. Stupid fool. You are no one's lord. You will die as will the witch Val—"

Turstin's fist connected with the side of Alfred's face and the unconscious body was dragged from the keep.

"What of the girl? The one he tortured?" Giles asked no one in particular but to him it seemed as if the world stilled while he waited for the answer.

"Vala lives. She is our birther," Editha said proudly.

She lived. The relief was sharp and sweet, and completely unwanted. Giles stepped off the dais and strode toward the group. She was nothing to him. He clenched his fists. "The land is fraught with problems." He paced in front of them. "The keep has been left to rot. I'll be living here and expect that some of you will as well as those that did in the past, cooks, steward, maids."

Silence.

"Is there one among you that cooks?"

"I was the cook before ..." Editha's voice trailed.

"You will cook here again. When I have a hut built for you, you and your family will move into the bailey."

"No, my lord."

"No?"

"There is—" Editha worried her lip and shuffled her feet.

"Evil," a girl piped behind her. "He is here."

Magna elbowed her way from the midst of the crowd. If she had been a man, Giles would have sworn she was taking his measure. She held out her hand. She wanted the stone. He heard her words for even though they were unspoken, their intent rang loud.

His hand moved almost against his will into the leather pouch secreted inside his tunic. His hand wrapped around the stone and it heated. He withdrew the stone, his will seemingly gone forced beneath some power she had exerted over him. He held it out and heard the collective gasp of indrawn breaths. She did not take it.

"It is as I thought. There is another half."

"What say you?"

"The women, they know. For to them it was entrusted."

She came so close to Giles he could touch her without reaching. He almost gagged at the smell of onions.

She smiled and then whispered, "That is all that grows here, my lord. You will get used to it."

Her face blurred and then became clear with full pouted lips and the clear skin of youth. Giles pinched his eyes closed and as quickly reopened them. Only a smelly old woman now stood before him.

She leaned toward him and poked a finger at his chest. "There is evil in this keep and now on this land." She closed his fingers around the stone. "Do not let go of the stone until the time is right and it joins with the other."

When he glanced up from the stone, the old woman, changeling creature, whatever she was, the one called Magna, had disappeared

The One. Your time has come.

This time the words seemed to echo from the palm of his hand where the stone still pulsed.

◆

Dark eyes beckoned to her. He lifted her as the crowd silently parted. Vala shuddered as a delicious ripple ran through her body. She had waited for him. His arms pulled her tight. She sighed and snuggled against his shoulder. He smelled of leather and wood smoke. He smelled like man. He smelled divine. She smiled and burrowed closer.

Who are you? She looked deep into his eyes searching for the answer. Dark eyes, Norman eyes yet not, for in their depths there was a hint of familiar blue.

The silence awoke her. It was naught but a dream. But who was he and why did she dream of him? Light glinted across the floor of the hut. She shivered. The fire was out. Vala groaned and attempted to roll over. Her muscles were raw and every movement was agony. Grimacing, she sat up on the straw pellet.

"He is the chosen."

The aged voice was the one constant in her life and always appeared at odd moments, unheralded but always welcome.

"It was not a dream?" Vala's voice was husky even to her own ear and her throat ached.

"He stopped the torture. He was the foil to the priest."

"He ...?" A spate of coughing stopped her speech.

"He is the reason you yet live. His name is Giles and he is the one. It is as it was told," Magna said confidently. "He and one other is your destiny."

Surely she had heard her wrong.

"Nay girl," the Ancient said. "You heard right."

"Rosaline?" she whispered and shuddered as she awaited the answer. She closed her eyes, her lids heavy. Magna's rough, gnarled hands stroked through the tangled mess of Vala's hair.

"No," Vala whispered as her shoulders begin to shake. "No," she whispered again. The aura of death swirled, its chill fog misting the earthen floor.

Vala, do not cry for me.

In another time, Vala's screams might have echoed through the village and into the keep but now her screams could only awaken the dead, for they were silent screams. They were screams that would have terrified the living, had they been heard.

Chapter Four

The scream rose loud, agonized and female. Giles jerked from his chair where he had been idly toying with his eating dagger. His hand curled around the hilt of his sword. He took in a breath, prepared to begin bellowing orders to his men who lounged in various parts of the hall and apparently oblivious to the scream of distress.

Were they all deaf? The scream was loud enough to wake the oldest crone in the keep.

Reality settled in the wake of the scream's echo. It had happened again like it had many times before. The agony of some soul, and only Giles was aware. Silently, he cursed his mother's gift, the sight. He touched the pouch.

"Jesu!"

He slammed his hand against his thigh. Pain shot up his arm and his burnt fingers throbbed. "God's tooth!" he muttered and jammed a forefinger into his mouth.

Royce looked up from where he was dicing with Robert. "What's wrong?"

"Nothing." Giles dropped his hand.

"Nothing?" Royce rose from the bench.

"Stay."

"You're certain?"

Giles shook his head. "I just need to stretch my legs. Go back to your dicing."

Royce shrugged his shoulders.

As Giles left the keep, the scream continued to echo in his ears. It was the girl the priest had tortured. He knew it with a certainty. Her name, he struggled to remember and all that came to him was the feel of her and the scent of lavender.

Vala. The name came from nowhere and everywhere.

"T'would be too much to ask you to show yourself?" he muttered. For in the short time he had been here, voices from nowhere had unfortunately become part of the norm. He strode into the bailey where he drew in gulps of fresh air morning air. The clean scent was a welcome relief from the hall where the odor of ancient grease, smoke and animal droppings still clung. His eyes roved the crumbling huts in the bailey. A lucky man Royce had called him only yesterday. He nodded at several of his men who were making disjointed efforts to repair the huts.

The cobbles trembled with life in the wake of the scream. She, Vala, called for him and his stride lengthened.

•

Usually the forest closed around Vala, comforted her. Not today. The crackle of broken twigs beneath her feet only fueled her anger and her determination.

He is the One.

The wind whispered through the trees. Vala leaned against one of the many huge oak trees. She slid her back down the tree trunk and pulled her knees to her chest.

The pool lay still, cobalt blue in the morning light. Its surface shimmered and reflected the peace Vala craved. She pulled off her tunic and left only the light, gauzy garment that she wore beneath. She edged a toe into the water. The sun shone warm on her face but the water was biting, cold. She waded into the center and dunked her head beneath the surface. Despite the cold, the water closed around her in a refreshing cocoon. She surfaced with a sigh. She had feared that the water punishment would have ended her enjoyment of the pond and that only fear would have remained. The pond was a haven where peace returned and logic could be sorted from the muddle of her thoughts.

Vala waded from the water and sat on the bank. She combed her dripping hair with her fingers and twisted the hem of the filmy undergarment with her hands. She rose and wandered farther from the edge of the pond.

Rosaline was dead. Babes continued to die. A Norman was in the keep. Could it get worse?

Anger washed over her in waves that put her off balance as the peace of the pond rapidly dissipated.

"Ayyyyh," she screamed her impotent fury into the Trees of Truth. Her hand tangled in her hair as she spun and screamed. Spent, she choked back a sob and sank to the ground.

"There is no time for pity, girl."

Vala wrapped her arms around her legs and rested her forehead on her knees. Leaves and twigs broke and crunched as footfalls moved around her. A breeze danced through the trees and lifted her hair gently from her neck.

"It is time," Vala reluctantly whispered.

"To let the anger go." Magna's voice held the strength of youth and the sureness of the ages.

"I need more time."

"There is none. As you already know." Ancient eyes swept over the telling glint of gold on Vala's hand. "You are not alone. The Ancients are with you, always."

"I know, but still it is only I."

"For now but soon Mervaine and the other Ancients will return."

Vala sighed. Eons had passed since the Ancients had physically left Hafne, although Vala could still feel their presence now and then by the pond where that final prophesy was revealed and the curse spoken.

Magna held out her hand and Vala clasped it. She felt the young, almost childlike softness of the Ancient's skin, for the Ancients were immortal but only Magna remained for now - the guide. Blue sparks flashed around the iron gray of Magna's hair and in the distance thunder began to collect in low belting booms in the distant horizon.

"Come, child."

Vala ran to keep up with Magna who appeared to glide over the forest floor. "Alfred?" she asked, hoping the false priest was really gone.

"Watch the shadows."

Vala nodded. In the few months he had lived in the village, things had gotten much worse. The livestock were all but gone. The howls at night had come closer and the women began to disagree constantly among themselves.

"He is the leader of the Others."

Vala started. It was unlike Magna to reveal so much. The Others, those with Norman blood, the missing men of Hafne.

"This prophecy is nearing an end," Magna nodded. "The evil has been set loose. He roams, but always he returns to the keep. As it is foretold, so it will be. Accept your destiny."

Go to him. Go to the Norman.

"But—" Vala stopped. She was alone. Magna had vanished.

But the forest wasn't empty and she was not alone.

"Magna?" Vala whispered and knew that it was not she.

Her throat constricted. Dark eyes, the scent of leather and wood smoke flooded her senses. The dream that awoke her only hours before came back in a rush. Reality faded.

Her feet slid forward hardly touching the ground. Again, his arms pulled her tightly against a strong chest. Again, she sighed and snuggled against his shoulder. He smelled like man. He smelled divine. She smiled and burrowed closer.

In the dream's trance she blindly glided.

•

The trees parted. Giles was not a religious man. He had no time for the foolish spouting of the local priests, conniving self-important fools like the one he had just banished from the village. He did not believe in apparitions or visions, religious or otherwise. Yet the creature that emerged from the forest in a silken wrap of gossamer could only be a vision.

Saints, but this was the holy lady herself, he thought.

White blond hair gleamed and wrapped a mystical robe around her slender figure. Elegant legs, bare legs, his mouth dried. The shift she wore was sheer enough to have been made by the angels. A warm glow of unreality filled the clearing.

His search for Vala was forgotten as he gazed on this magical, yet very earthy creature. He moved slowly so as not to frighten her. For surely something so fey would disappear as quickly as she'd appeared. Her gauzy covering shimmered in the dim glow of the forest light. It fluttered and twisted as if in the wake of a gentle breeze. He knew instinctively that her limbs shook.

Why was she here in the forest in a sheer tunic made to seduce? If not to be seduced, what else? It was a simple garment, and he knew there was naught else beneath. For he could see the outline of her breasts and the rise of her nipples as the sheer film of material sculpted them. As if she knew his thoughts, she crossed her arms protectively across her chest.

He reached out to her. She looked up with eyes rich with secrets. Small white teeth pearled over her bottom lip and a warm blush colored her high cheekbones. He brushed a tendril of velvet soft hair from her face. A creature of the forest that was causing an unsought earthly reaction and all he could think of was release. He pulled her to him.

A breeze lifted the leaves that had crumbled beneath his feet. Small broken pieces danced around them. That same breeze molded the filmy garment to her body. His hand skimmed her ribs. He felt her heart beat wildly beneath his hand. Felt the warmth of her body and the fragileness of her frame. She raised her lips to him, an offering he couldn't refuse. They were sweet with the scent of lavender as they moved softly, seductively against his. He pulled her tighter and his hand lightly grazed her breast. The sigh that escaped her urged him to possess her further. His tongue toyed with hers. Blood pounded in his ears.

It had been so long, too long. Heat pulsed, heated until it burned unbearably. The heat took flight as his mind awoke—the stone! He let her go.

She looked at him with an awareness that startled him. It was as if she knew everything about him... Impossible!

"Who are you?" He immediately regretted the harsh bite of his words.

The vision was slipping away from him, leaving his arms empty. For a brief moment she paused, looked back at him with jaded wisdom in her dark blue eyes then darted into the depths of the forest.

Giles dragged in air and gulped it back. His breath came fast and rough. What had happened? Never had he had such a reaction. Never had the stone reacted for no reason, and he could see none. There was no premonition, nothing. True, he had never toyed with a creature of the forest. A fairy.

Ridiculous!

He did not believe much in fairies even though the stone continued to pulse uncomfortably warm against his thigh.

•

Vala returned to the pond. She dragged the back of her hand across her mouth. The tingle would not stop. She scrubbed her lips.

The passion that had possessed her mother as easily as the magic had guided her was clearly now Vala's. It had ruined her mother, destroyed her gifts. Was she more like her mother than she had known?

She picked her tunic up from the ground. She pulled it over her body and tried to forget the places his hands had touched. It had been him, the wretched Norman. The One. Giles, they called him. Her hands trembled as she thought of the passion that must be and yet, had flamed too easily. Despite the reading of the runes, or the foretelling of dreams, passion would not control her heart. She was stronger than that.

There was not much time before the Helios, the eclipse of the sun that preceded the full moon. It was a precarious time for everyone but especially those that were chosen. Vala knew that her destiny could also mean her death.

Would the Norman accept his destiny and possibly his own death?

She clung to the anger and rose to quit the place where before she had once only found peace. Her heart beat loud and fast. Her tongue skimmed her lips that still tingled, rough and swollen from his kisses. She glared into the gray sky and spoke to the heavens.

"Mayhap he is the one." She gritted her teeth. "The one to die!"

Behind her the wind howled.

•

"Follow the Norman, you fool." Alfred spat. He reached inside his robe and scratched his crotch.

"But," the creature called Ewaldo whined.

"There is no time."

The creature's presence reminded him of the mistake. He had let the creature kill the lustful Norman, a stranger the girl Rosaline had met outside the village. Since that kill, the creature's bloodlust had become insatiable.

Even though it was the spawn of the Rogue, he eyed the thing with distaste. He knew that the Rogue needed an heir to regain his lost immortality. He didn't know why that was possible. He only knew it was. He also knew that the Rogue lived only because of the bodies he stole before they breathed their last. He'd hop skipped through centuries moving from one body to another. Alfred knew no more, but he did know the only living thing the Rogue could find before his last body died—was unwilling.   Unwilling and unnatural, and the result would walk the earth indefinitely seeking release.

Alfred clutched his scalp as pain shot through his brain, the memories of the master continued to overlay his own. The images flashed through his mind. It had taken many centuries before the sun completely disappeared from the earth again, before the moment was exactly right.

He turned his attention back to the creature. "Ewaldo, under no circumstance must you kill for that will draw attention to us. We can't chance it especially now when the Normans provide all the diversion we need to begin our work. Follow the new Norman lord. I need to know what he is about."

Chapter Five

"Vala, what is it? You look ill." Esma met Vala as she returned to the village.

"I went to him," she whispered. "I don't know why."

"The new lord? He is the one. That is why." Esma paused. "But you know that. For that is why you are drawn to him. Tis not just because of his good looks."

Vala believed her for Esma also had a gift and could occasionally pick up on the signals of the Ancients. Like Vala, and so many other women in the village, she also had Ancient blood.

She took Vala's hand and drew her closer. "Do you know that when we went to the keep Magna was there?"

"What happened?" Vala asked and shivered.

"Magna went toward the Norman and held out her hand. The air seemed overly warm then as if a number of candles flickered in the air between them. Like light and warmth all together. I have shivers up and down my backbone even now just thinking about it. It is hard to explain, but he knew what she wanted and opened a pouch that he keeps hidden beneath his tunic."

"I was not far behind Magna so I saw much. He had a stone." Esma stopped and placed a hand to her mouth. Her eyes were round with fright. "It pulsed. Pulsed … like the other did."

The seer's stone! Impossible! Vala's heart beat so rapidly a dull pain seemed to fill her chest.

She grasped Esma's hand in both of hers but her thoughts were in turmoil and would not allow her to project any feelings of reassurance. The seer's stone, the second half returned by a man, a Norman man. Was it possible? Was he part of the prophecy? Was he the chosen, carrying the blood of the three, Saxon, Ancient and Norman? Was he the one or was he just another Norman marauder?

She dropped Esma's hands.

"Your destiny?" Esma asked quietly but her fingers trembled as she bunched the hem of her tunic.

Vala nodded seriously. "I'll need the ring pouch."

Esma frowned. "What do ye plan?"

"The day has come."

Overhead, the sunshine-streaked clouds belied the recent rains that left the ground dry.

Esma grabbed Vala's hand. Together they walked through the village toward the hut that Esma shared with her mother.

Hidden deep beneath the corner post of Esma's hut, the leather sack was dull with dirt. Reverently Vala lifted it from its hiding place. It seemed unbelievable to her that finally now, with the keep overrun with Normans, the time had arrived.

She pulled on the fraying hemp. The knot fell open with ease after years where it had been weakened by rot. Within the nest of dirt and leather, gold gleamed as richly as it had at its inception. Vala slid the ring on her finger. "The truth will be known should the Norman have a like ring."

"Through the generations our heritage passed through two women of separate blood, yet each carried the blood of the three: Saxon, Norman, Ancient. The ring has passed through them to remind us of who we are and what Hafne shall be. This you know."

"Hidden only after the final betrayal and with the return of the Rogue," Esma added. "For he is here and we locked the keep against him."

"Aye. And the Norman dog has set him free." Vala drew a line in the dirt. "I have dreamt of him twice."

"The Norman?"

"Aye."

Vala rose and silently embraced Esma before turning to leave.

"Vala," Esma called.

But Vala left the hut without a backward look and began to run. Her bare feet flew across the rough meadow grass. In the woods she stopped, her breathing light, her heart heavy. Magna's words came back to her as they had again and again since that fateful day.

"Vala, you are the last of your mother's line. Their blood must not die," Magna had said, then pressed the ring into her hands. "Hide the ring separate from your piece of the parchment. Your destiny will be met when the Rogue returns. In twos and threes it will happen. Wait for the signs."

It had always been Magna, and the shadow of the Ancients that hovered on the periphery of her life since that day when she had arrived, a bedraggled waif clinging to her mother's hand. Wulfgar, the last Saxon leader, had taken them in and immediately her mother became his mistress. It was the only way he would let them stay. Her mother had wanted only protection for her child. It was a year later when Wulfgar and her mother died and the curse had begun.

•

It had taken her a day to gather the courage to come here. But now as Vala peered through the chinks of the stable, her fingers dug at the knothole. She could see nothing. She glanced over her shoulder and then rounded the corner of the stable. She flattened herself against the wall and ducked down.

Norman soldiers milled in the bailey, some engrossed in a game of dice. Lackwits! But the main activity was at the front of the keep by the palisade as the few village men worked to remove broken and rotted timbers. Impotent anger raged through her at what she saw, Saxons overseen by Normans.

But there was something else that warred with the anger as she thought of one man. She had felt the connection even when she had first opened her eyes, breathed air instead of water, and seen her rescuer. Giles they called him. She pinched her fingers together and still they trembled.

She turned her attention to today's quest. She had thought the deserted stable the best place for her beloved palfrey. Where she was away from the woods. She had come often and ridden her daily, until now, until the Norman's arrival.

In the stable Merva was safe for what killed in the shadows of the forest would not enter the confines of the keep. That is, she had been safe until the arrival of the Norman.

Vala's eyes shifted to the keep. Secrets cloaked the aged edifice, secrets that affected everyone's destiny. Within the stable she heard the rustle of straw as the horse settled in her stall.

"You are a beauty. Who do you belong to? If only you could speak."

Only concern for her palfrey kept Vala from running, running far from the dangerous pleasure of that voice. Instead she crept closer. She peered between the slats of wood. It was he, the Norman – the leader, the one who had tried to seduce her. She jerked back. That was a lie. He had not tried to seduce her. It had been she who had led the seduction. It was she who had followed what she thought was destiny. It would never happen again and yet it must.

Merva tossed her head and whinnied, sensing Vala's presence.

It took everything she had to attain calm. She directed her thoughts elsewhere.

It is all right my beauty. I'll come back later in the dark of night while the Norman sleeps. Vala projected to the mare.

The horse quieted as Vala knew she would.

She crept away. The Norman would care for Merva. She had no fear now for her horse's safety. She had seen his gentle sureness with the animal. She sidled toward the outside perimeter of the palisade meaning to slide through the gap she had entered through. There was no one around and she hid behind a cart waiting for an opportunity to bolt. But her attention was distracted as pain shot through her—intense hatred, vivid, alive, and yet as suddenly—gone.

•

Hidden high in the crumbling confines of the veiled third tower, eyes watched avidly. With years of practice he stilled his aura—an art he had learned many years ago when he was left to fend for himself. His mouth flattened in a hard line as he remembered when he was banished, Hafne's greatest hope. They had stolen his name because he had killed the whore that was his mother. But he had gotten back. He had cursed everything they loved. Still, hate pulsed hot, hard and dangerously near the surface.

He raised his hand, grimacing at the slight shake still present in the tips of his fingers from the effort of making his body energy go so still.

A glint of sunlight on steel drew his attention back to the courtyard. Light flickered briefly in his flat, dark eyes and then was gone.

◆

Vala shivered. She glanced up toward the two towers but there was nothing. Still, she had goose bumps.

She jumped as a hand clamped on her shoulder. It was him… only him, the Norman. The relief was fleeting as she was dragged into the threat of the present.

She could see from his eyes that he did not recognize her. Why would he? She did not resemble the waif he had attempted to seduce yesterday. Yet she knew that both the waif at the pond and the woman who stood before him were nothing to him, only objects on which to sate his desires.

"Who are you?" His heavy brows rose high to almost disappear beneath a fringe of thick dark chestnut hair that fell across his forehead. His lips were full but not lush. They suited him. She wanted to kiss him. She … She wished him to the peridition of Hades. Aye, she did.

She crossed her arms across her chest. And still, she quivered. There was something about him, something in his gaze, something in his presence. Something that drew her and she only wanted to step closer.

She took a step back.

Except for the amused angle of his eyebrow, his face was harsh, carved not unlike the stone that sheltered the pond, a solid persistent mask - a warrior's face. That was all, and she would never be drawn to that. She drew in a deep breath. He was nothing. He was Norman. And she only wanted to spit in that face, to grind her heel into his richly shod foot. She wanted to make him squirm, make him ache and feel as she had, as she did. As much as she was drawn to him, she drew as far away as his grip would allow.

"Release me," she commanded and surprisingly he did.

Vala twisted the thick gold ring and tried to still the trembling at the back of her knees. She stopped as she felt his eyes on her fingers.

He reached for her ring finger. The insignia glinted in the sunlight. He would not recognize the meaning, for the words came from the Ancients.

"Where did you get this?" Astonishment showed for a split second in his dark eyes.

"It was my mother's," she said, pulling her hand free.

"There were two."

The One, Vala ... the One...

Vala shook her head trying to free herself of the Ancient's damning echoes.

His proud tanned face leaned down so there were only inches between them. And she wanted nothing but to feel his lips on hers. She looked away.

"Who are you?" he said in a husky whisper.

"Vala," she muttered with childish defiance that shadowed the words and fought thoughts of his lips so damningly near.

"Vala." Her name fell easily from his lips. "Vala, the birther."

"How do you know that?"

"It is why you were being punished, is it not? You interfered with the priest."

"He wanted to cleanse."

"No matter."

"It matters greatly. He and the others seek to destroy the women." Vala drew herself up to her full height and glared at him. "The reason is everything. A woman is dead."

"Why would he seek to destroy the women? Without them there will be no future, no babes, no hope."

"It is more than that. The women are not just breeders," Vala said.

"Are they not?"

"Women will find peace here," she said and then pinched her lips in a tight line because already she'd said too much.

"There is much that remains untold. Eventually you will tell me all."

"When the time is right." She turned to leave him but she did not get far.

"Halt!" The voice boomed across the bailey and other heads turned to see what was going on.

Vala stopped. The authority in the voice would not allow otherwise.

He strode toward her and closed the distance in seconds. Standing in front of her, he blocked her view of the rest of the yard.

She felt his confusion as emotions twisted within him and then a mist clouded her inner vision and blocked everything.

"It was you," he whispered. "It was you in the forest. At the pond, Vala."

And then her lips were trapped beneath his and there was nothing she could do to stop the sweet torture. She gave him everything before her lips were freed as suddenly as they were captured.

And she wondered what had actually happened. How much he knew? And for the first time since the Norman had arrived, fear replaced the anger. He was everything she had ever dreamed of and everything she dreaded. He was Norman.

Chapter Six

This time when she turned to run there was no one to stop her. Vala did not stop until she was free from the bailey. She didn't stop until the light closed around her, and only glinted from the thick canopy of oak and yew trees overhead.

"The days shorten," Magna called cheerfully as she appeared beside a nearby tree.

The air shook as a wind began to howl.

Magna lifted her hand and the wind stopped.

"Do not doubt yourself. You are not like your mother."

Vala felt the flush film her cheekbones at what only yesterday the Norman had done, what she had let him do - wanted. She shivered at the thought of his hands on her body and his lips on hers.

"Some things are meant to be and some not." Magna swung the gnarled wood staff around her head and the air crackled as small sparks flew overhead.

"I am not ready," Vala said and knew she had no choice. She would never be ready.

"Your mother's death was a link in the chain that must be forged. This you know. If you follow your destiny, the curse will be broken this moon."

Magna disappeared before her last words faded.

Vala rubbed her forearms as a distant cackle floated through the air. "You are not always right. No matter, at least this time you are not."

Magna's image floated faintly in front of her.

The clouds parted and raindrops began to patter around her.

Magna's image continued to fade in and out. "I am always right, child, and you." She pointed her staff at Vala and the air around her popped. "You are now not the only one that has made their way to this pond. Together you have both been here in this forest, you, the Norman and no one else. For they, the Others, can't. Not yet. Why is that do you think?" Light crackled in the air around her as Magna faded into nothing.

•

Giles remained in the entrance to the keep long after Vala had disappeared. The minx had placed a spell on him!

Nay! Magic spells were only tales told to children.

But he had dreamt of her and in the depths of that dream she had loved him. And today the desire had been there. It was as if the dream had been a prophecy. He shook his head as if that would disspell the notion. Instead a chill snaked down his spine as he slipped for a brief second into the magic of the dream.

He was not naive. The desire that raged between them would not end. Unlike the magic, it couldn't be willed away. He knew naught of destiny but their bed sport would be satisfying for already the desire was there for both. He was in need of a wife. It was too bad that she was Saxon.

He thumbed the seer's stone. The old hag's image flirted in the dark edges of his memory.

You must choose. You are long awaited.

This place was like no other for until he had arrived here he had been able to ignore the abilities that marked him as different. But the magic that he had tried to deny all his life was steeped into every stone on his new land.

The sight, his healing aura and the damnable stone were all tools of magic. He had enough magic. He yanked his hand from his pouch and dropped it to his belt where he ran a finger over his dagger.

Vala was a tempting little minx and naught else. She would not change his destiny nor lead him with desire. No, nothing would change his destiny and that was building this keep and this land into the best fiefdom in England. It would be a fiefdom where magic would have no place and no fertile ground in which to root. This he vowed with every breath of his being.

He strode into the keep where he climbed the stairs to the

second floor.

He had barely reached the bedchamber when agony seared through his bones. Pain and grief tore through him. The sight stole his will as images flashed in his mind. Blood, and the immediacy of a battle scene drove out any remaining thoughts of magic or his long ago childhood. The roar of men in the midst of a battles rage, the screams of frightened horses and dying men filled his senses. Edward's face flooded his mind. He held out his hand to Giles, blood dripping from his mailed hand.

Giles sucked in air in a painful hitch. "Edward," he breathed to the knight who was the closest thing to a brother Giles would ever know.

The image blurred with blood as Mathilde's face overlaid Edward's. The pain slashed through Giles with raw agony. Blindly he reached his hand out to the image of his anguished friend's woman. The image was so vivid that it was like she stood before him.

"Mathilde!" he yelled. "Nay!"

"What is it?" Royce roared as he raced up the steps. "What did you see?"

"Nothing."

"Nothing? You yelled Mathilde's name. She is not here."

"Go!" he fought to keep his voice steady. "Leave me."

Royce hesitated.

Giles swallowed heavily. "Send for her."

"Aye." Royce nodded and left him.

•

He crawled slowly down the broken ladder from the tower, his head awhirl with thoughts. The witch had tried to hide the truth from him those many years ago. His lips drew back in a snarl.

Flesh of his flesh walked the earth. For years he had tried and failed to achieve the immortality that was stolen from him. But she had been here all this time hidden by the Ancient. He sneered. The Ancients would never return. He had won. For with her by his side he would have everything. Hafne would be his. The truth nearly blinded him. For the truth lay in the yellow of gold he had waited to see for so many years. It was the gold of a ring so ancient that even the Ancients did not remember its true origin.

Chapter Seven

The next day, Giles' strode across the short span between the bailey and the edge of the village. There was no one in sight. Unlike the lush woods that surrounded the village, the land here was barren. Not even a cow grazed in the fields. Despite the rain that he knew had ravaged the land not so many days ago, the ground was hard and dry.

The desolation only made Giles more determined to make this fiefdom the most prosperous in all of England. To do that he knew that he must gain the people's trust. Not a simple feat. Yet his gut told him that the hag and Vala knew much.

He was in front of the hut where he had first carried her, Vala. It was hard to forget. Small and beaten, somehow worse than the rest, it was a miserable excuse for shelter. It was harder to forget her for he could still taste her sweetness.

He thumped on the door, waited patiently for all of a moment and then shouldered the door open. It swung easily and he stumbled, and almost fell into the room.

Inside, the hut was sterile, devoid of the smell of food or human activity. Damp spring air wept from the cracks in the walls and ran in rivulets to the dirt floor. Yet outside the ground was bone dry. He squatted before the fire pit, trailing his fingers through ashes that sifted dry and cold between his fingers.

"She is not here."

Giles' hand rested on the hearth ashes as he swiveled to face the old woman, Magna.

"You must go to her."

Giles rose but even from his height advantage he felt like a small boy before her, like he had at the knee of his mother as she tried to teach him the power of her magic. He cleared his throat trying to rid himself of the discomfort that shrouded him. Images dashed before him, Magna, as he had once known her.

"I know you." The words involuntarily leapt from him. Uncharacteristic of him for always he thought before he acted, but somehow it was not unexpected here in this place.

"Do you?"

The memory flitted and sharpened in the forefront of his mind. "You were with my mother, at the end."

The old woman only smiled at him.

He started. What was he saying? His mother had left him when he was very small.

"Who are you?"

But the old woman was already gone.

Go to her.

His hand reached for the pouch and he rubbed the stone absently.

Vala.

The old woman's voice hung in the cool air.

"Vala," Giles repeated.

"'Tis me but you knew that."

He swung around. Vala stood in the doorway and even in the dim light was beautiful. Her breasts rose high and firm, and she was not a dream. *Nay*, he thought. *She must be a dream.* For she was everything he had dreamt of. He dragged his gaze to her face and was trapped by blue eyes that spoke of secrets, promises and more. There was a vulnerability there like there had been that unforgettable day when he had not recognized her. When she had come to him like a wood nymph within the forest. He swallowed heavily. He couldn't think of the forest.

"Come here," she commanded and held out her hand.

He couldn't stop himself and even if he could, he didn't want to. He gave her his hand so that she could lead him like a small child.

"Where?" he asked thickly.

She stopped and trailed a delicate finger along his upper arm.

"No," he said, for the sensation was beyond words. He was acting like a boy who had never seen a woman. He pulled her toward him and kissed her. The taste of her was oddly sweet, and he never wanted to stop.

"Stop," she commanded against his lips but her breasts lightly grazed his chest and he could only cup her face and kiss her deeper. But when his hand dipped and cupped a firm breast, and his finger traced the rapidly hardening nipple, he knew he was done. Saxon or no, she would be his. But as that thought slipped through his mind, pain shot through his foot.

"Jesu!" He roared and leapt back, his foot aching from the weight of her heel hitting his instep. "What did I do to you?"

"Do to you? You took liberties, my lord."

"Giles."

She drew herself up, straight and tall. And he drew his gaze away from the place where his hands had last been.

"I have work to do this day. Good day, my lord, Giles."

•

Silently he followed her. That he limped from the injury she had imposed on his foot, mattered not. Vala walked with her head high like he didn't exist. Ahead a group of young women were gathered around the well. She caught a thread of their conversation.

"He'll move us all back to the keep."

A full bucket sloshed against the well.

"Here," Vala hissed, motioning Giles as she grasped the edge of a nearby cart and slid into the shadows. She knew they would mind their words in her presence. She needed them to speak freely, so she hid. She stilled her aura. The faint hum of that living light was quickly silent. She trembled as she struggled to contain it, and almost lost all will as he pushed tightly against her, as his forearm met hers, hard and warm and... She took a deep breath.

"Shhh!" she put a finger to her lips as she shifted away from him.

He moved closer. "Why are we hiding?" he whispered back. His hand softly brushed her cheek.

"Don't. Not here. Not now. Please."

"Ahh, she begs."

His warm breath fanned her ear in a caress that made her ache for more. Instead, she glared at him.

"The smith, even the foul priest, warned them against opening the keep. But they would not listen." The same woman who had spoken earlier, Anne, persisted.

"He is lord."

"So he says." Anne's voice was full of disdain.

"He is there. The Rogue. I felt it. He will not rest until we answer to him, or die."

"Of who do they speak?" Giles asked softly.

His lips grazed her ear and she quivered in a combination of fear and desire.

She held up her hand. "Stop."

Vala's head hurt and she began to lose track of which voice belonged to who. The prophecy was descending on them. Everything in her body screamed to run, to leave this place and this time, and everything in her heart kept her feet planted where they were.

"He is our new lord. Mayhap he can break the curse." There was hope in Esma's voice.

"Mayhap. Sometimes I think there wouldn't be a curse if it weren't for Vala." Anne said. "The crops grew until her arrival."

"That's not true and you know it. Do you not remember how it was before? Remember the stories of the elders. The Normans were here long before our time. You only need look to your mother, half Norman she is. The Normans arrived thrice. The first time ended Hafne as the Ancients knew it those many eons ago."

Vala smiled. Esma was always loyal.

"Aye," another agreed. "Because the one they now call Rogue murdered his own mother."

"Jesu," Giles murmured.

Vala took his hand and squeezed, reminding him to be silent. He squeezed back and his thigh brushed against hers. She let go of his hand. She must pay attention and forget that only mere cloth separated his flesh from hers.

"True," Esma agreed. "And he cursed the land as Mervaine the eldest of the Ancients took immortal life and his name from him. But there is more. Rosaline sought to end it before Hafne was no more."

"Or the Rogue takes us all," another murmured.

"But never Vala. She is one of the chosen," Esma said stoutly. "And Rosaline she meant well."

"Rosaline." Anne chortled bitterly. "By laying with a Norman. Silly whore."

The slap rang through the stillness.

With her hand over her cheek, Anne ran. She stopped a few feet from Vala. Her hand dropped to her side, revealing the pink imprint of Esma's hand. "Because of you and yours," she said viciously. A drop of spittle formed on her lips before dropping to the ground. "Already you side with him!" She pointed at Giles.

"Nay, you are so wrong." Vala turned her back on Anne and was brought short by the frightened faces on the rest of the women. Vala walked quickly toward them but they gathered their full water buckets.

But their fear was overwhelming as Vala closed her eyes and drew inward. With a forefinger centered on her forehead, she took a deep breath just as Magna had taught her. With only the power of her mind she used her aura to control theirs and smoothed their anger and fear into stillness. A wave of calm entered their auras as they quickly hurried away.

"Cease this nonsense," Giles commanded.

"You shouldn't do that," Esma said as she slid up beside her. "My lord," she murmured to Giles.

"They were past mere words. Later I'll speak to each of them but it would have been pointless now," Vala said and glanced at Giles. So it would be like that. He would accept the desire between them but not the power of the magic. That made it all so much more difficult. T'was just like a man.

"You have heard about Rosaline?" Esma broke into her thoughts.

"I am so sorry ..."

Esma caught Vala's hand. "Rosaline died of a broken heart. It was out of your control. She chose the Norman to end the curse and fell in love. No one could have prevented her death."

"Blood of the three. The babe was not meant to be." Vala said. Esma frowned and looked at Giles.

"Tis all right. Magna says he must know."

"What is this hocus pocus?" Giles stood up and faced Esma.

"Tis not hocus pocus," Esma snapped. She swung to Vala. "You have much work if this—" She stabbed a finger at Giles. "—is your destiny."

"Of what do you speak?" Giles demanded. "You speak nonsense. Destiny, curse, blood of the three. Ignorance. All of it."

Esma turned to Vala as if Giles had never spoken. "She loved him."

"I'll miss her."

"As will I. She was my sister." Esma dropped Vala's hand and wiped at her eyes. "But she is with them now, the Norman and her babe. I can only think she is happy."

"Both of you will cease this talk." Giles faced Vala. "You, will follow me to the keep, now."

"Nay, my lord," Vala said firmly. "Anon, but not now."

"I could force you."

"Aye, you could. T'would do you no good."

He glared at her, the passion flirting dangerously close to the surface of his dark blue eyes. She looked away.

"Within the hour," he commanded. "And you will tell me who this Rogue is amongst other things."

"He is only hocus pocus," Vala replied.

"As I expected. One hour," he commanded before striding away.

"The battle has begun," Vala whispered to Esma and crossed her arms as if that would calm the thumping of her heart. She watched Giles disappear into the baily.

"He may be Norman but ..." Esma giggled. "Bedding him t'would not be a hardship."

"Don't. Tis not the time." Vala glanced behind her. "I see things in the shadows where there is nothing."

"Do you think Alfred is finally gone?" Esma whispered becoming immediately serious. "The other women are even afear'd to speak his name, that it might evoke him. I do not care what anyone says, he was one of the Others."

Vala's aura trembled. Instinctively she knew the energy came from the keep. Deep within the broken ruins of that long ago first tower, he lived.

Chapter Eight

Smoke curled from the keep. Vala thought of the Normans, warm and safe in the great hall and her thumb nail bit into her palm. She was here at his command. Giles. Her pace quickened and the hastily attached wimple flapped in the breeze. Wisps of hair escaped and fluttered around her face. Norman soldiers hooted from their guard duty on the ramparts.

"Pretty one, come up here."

"We have something for you."

She glared back but any retort was interrupted as another Norman touched her arm.

The Norman grinned through broken teeth. Today he took liberties he had never before attempted. His hand roughly grasped her breast.

Vala didn't think. Her reaction was instinctive when she punched him.

He dropped back howling piteously. "I was only wanting a bit of fun."

Norman dogs! Her teeth clenched. She would speak to Giles. She would not be treated thus and neither would any of the other women. This was not England, think what they might, the Norman bastards. They had conquered England. This was Hafne and it belonged to the Ancients.

She thought of Giles and she hesitated, her stride shortened. He was different in ways that even Magna had not forseen. And he tempted her like no man ever had. She shuddered and drew her cloak tighter around her. She was not at his command. She had other tasks to see to before she obeyed him. Obey, she gritted her teeth and yet she shivered at the thought of him. She had no time for the feelings that pulsed through her at the mere thought of him. Such nonsense only confused her and blurred her destiny.

She veered right, away from the keep. It was only a short walk to Nelda's hut. The hut was solid, more secure than many in the village, for Nelda's husband was a woodworker.

Vala ducked through the low entrance. She blinked in the dimness. A candle flickered feebly on the table.

Vala shivered. The hut was damp, cool and the fire was out. The woman was sleeping, her arms bare, her pregnant belly jutting against her worn tunic. Vala bent and picked up the sacking from the floor and drew it over Nelda. The woman shifted. Vala prayed the babe would live. There hadn't been a live birth in the village in over eight years.

Vala ducked as she exited the hut and her gaze immediately drew to the edges of the forest. She stood for a few minutes before walking toward the other women who waited patiently for word of Nelda.

"Nelda? The babe?" Editha asked her immediately.

"She is fine as is the babe. Nelda is resting. The babe is restless and seems determined to come before its time. I hope she'll rest these next few months. With the gods' will, the babe will wait."

"If the birth reaches term it will pass the time of the full moon," Willa's face lit with hope. "Do you think it is possible?"

Anne sneered. "The babe will die like the others."

"Do not say that!" Aedre exclaimed. "Do not say that. Do not even think it. Even if it were true."

"It is not," said Willa firmly. "Vala will end the curse. I know she will."

"I'll make it happen," Vala agreed, stubbornly lifting her chin. "The curse will be broken. In the meantime, as intolerable as it may seem, we must accept the Norman."

"So we are agreed," Editha said. "We'll accept the Norman's leadership." The words were strained, for humility did not come easy to her, not to the gods she worshiped and certainly not for a man. Her smile was crooked. "At least some of it."

The women all nodded.

"But we'll not make his life too easy," Esma vowed.

"It goes without saying that he must learn who holds the power in Hafne. But first we must bathe. I can't tolerate this another minute," Editha said firmly.

"Thank the gods. I did not know how much longer I can stand the stench," Esma groaned.

Editha scratched discreetly under her arm. "I agree with Esma. I can hardly stand it myself." She wrinkled her nose. "I doubt if I'll ever get the smell from the hut."

Editha and the other women had not bathed in over a month, ever since the runes had been thrown and the future read by Willa. When the women of Hafne had learned of the imminent arrival of the Normans they had hoped that the dilapidated keep and barren land, combined with filthy uncooperative people, would discourage the Normans. It was a plan Vala, as birther couldn't participate in.

"One of the Norman dogs wrestled me just outside the gates yesterday," Aedre said. "Were it not that we were not alone, who knows what might have happened."

"That will not be born. I'll end it now." Vala wheeled around and marched toward the keep.

•

Giles swung the hammer against the rock, shattering it to make new cobbles to replace the bailey's worn and partially missing ones. The work was much needed but for him it was also an attempt to keep his mind from Vala. It was futile. She was everything he had always wanted in a woman—beautiful, intuitive. Yet, she was also Saxon. Or was she? And where was she? He looked up. The sun had shifted in the sky. It had been at least two hours since he commanded her here.

He wiped sweat from his brow with the back of his hand. She was respected, a leader in the village. Odd, women did not lead in any society he had ever seen and he had seen many in his travels over the continent.

"Take her to bed. That will take your mind off things," Royce said as they took a short break. "Tis what I always do. No woman is worth that look."

"No woman caused the look," Giles shot back.

"No?"

"Not wholly." Giles smiled. "You're right, a night of sport should settle the matter."

"Could not have said it better." Royce leaned on his sledge. "Jesu! Tis blistering hot this day."

"Aye, for spring no less. And it rained last night."

"You would hardly know it. The ground is dry." Royce scuffed it with his boot. "This place is more than uncommonly strange." He glanced behind him and nudged Giles, smiling. "But the women are uncommonly fair."

Giles followed Royce's gaze and saw Vala hurrying along. As usual her braid was loose beneath her wimple and her fair hair flew across her face. He did not want whatever discussion she had in mind, not today for it was obvious that it was not just his command that brought her here. Even from here he could feel her determination and if that wasn't enough, the small hands fisted at her side told him everything he needed to know. And despite his earlier command, he hoped against hope that her destination was elsewhere other than him. He turned back to his work and raised the sledge over his shoulder.

•

Giles' broad back was bare and glistened with sweat. Her temper rose in tandem with the attraction she so desperately tried to avoid.

The Norman she had hit only a short while earlier trotted beside her. "Kiss me," he crowed and puckered his lips close to her face. She cuffed him and was rewarded with an exaggerated howl.

Ahead she saw that Giles had laid the sledge aside.

"Be gone!" she commanded fighting for control.

"Pretty." He stroked her arm.

She pulled away. It was apparent his brain was addled but still he annoyed her, his unwanted attention combined with the other men's lack of respect was just too much.

"Leave me!" she demanded.

"Gilroy, you have work to do."

The words filled the bailey, easy, authoritative and so very masculine.

Gilroy laughed and ran off.

"This must cease at once," she said when she was face to face with Giles. "He humiliates the women."

"He can't help himself. He has never been right since taking a mace to the head."

"He is not the only one who harries the women."

"Harries? You have been much sheltered here. You know not

your woman's place."

"Place. Woman's place!" Her voice rose.

He calmly stroked his chin but his nostrils flared despite his languid movements.

"There is no humor in this situation. I demand you do something!"

The smile he had been hiding swept across the strong planes of his face. He chuckled. "I find much humor."

"The women are frightened. Is this what you wanted?"

"Frightened? That is not possible. Surely, they know it is only in fun."

"This was our land and it is not like yours. Women had respect."

"Respect?" he repeated, his brow furrowed.

Respect. The word echoed around the bailey passing amidst the Normans. "Respect!" She jabbed a finger at him and then at the men behind him. "Instead they hurl insults."

"Insults? Such as?"

"That—never mind."

"You are fair of face, mayhap." His brows arched and his lip twitched again. "Tis true and hardly an insult."

"Your men make the women uncomfortable."

"I'll speak to them." The corners of his eyes crinkled.

She would blister him if he laughed.

"It is worse than mere words. One of your men grappled with Aedre yesterday."

The twitch was gone. "Was she hurt?"

A slim dark-haired man pushed up beside Giles. "Aedre. She was not hurt?"

Vala had heard him called Turstin.

"Nay, there were too many around for much damage to be done. Still if she'd been alone, who knows what could have happened." Vala glanced between Giles and the second Norman.

"Who did this?" Turstin's fists clenched.

"She is not hurt but—" Vala began.

"There are no buts," Giles broke in. "Turstin, leave. I'll handle this. The women will not be bothered any longer."

"You can be sure of it," Turstin muttered as he backed away.

"You will be safe. My men will behave from hence forth," Giles addressed Vala seriously like there had never been a passionate moment between them. Like they were distant strangers. "You have my word."

He wheeled and strode away. The noise in the bailey quickly returned to a normal level as without words, his lead was followed. The other men fell in step with him and the clatter of iron on stone filled the bailey.

Vala swung around and began to march through the gates but froze before she had taken many steps. Iron gates that had been broken and rusted were replaced with solid untarnished iron bars. She remembered the sound of the forge roaring through the night hours. Much had been completed in a very short time. The Norman was not so useless. Not so useless at all.

It was unsettling.

•

A figure slithered through the shadows. His rough bony hands clenched and unclenched. The urge to kill was strong but the call of his master stopped him. He ran toward the call putting into the pounding efforts of his feet all the pent up frustration of not attaining the release of a kill. Maybe later he'd take a cow or a goat, maybe both. Ewaldo licked his lips and his breath fogged the warm air.

Chapter Nine

The early morning sun struggled to rise in the cloud-studded sky. Its timid rays highlighted the shadows that flitted around the pair who now roamed the cliff edge.

"As I feared," Alfred said as he stroked his chin.

"I'll tell him," Ewaldo snarled.

Alfred whirled on him. "You will not!"

"Yes, but the master will be angry if we do not tell." Ewaldo scratched his throat and left red tracks along the skin beneath the dark stubble. He jerked his sharp head toward the keep. "The Norman is the one."

Alfred dragged a hand across his chin. Should the master learn of this his own death would be immediate. The curse must not be broken. The two must be kept apart.

"You will say nothing," Alfred snarled.

"What is there for me?"

"I'll let you kill the girl."

"When?" Ewaldo licked his thin lips.

"Soon. Before the moon turns. She'll be yours."

Saliva dripped from Ewaldo's pointed chin as if already tasting the warm salt of her blood.

•

The mist hung low over waves that battered the rocks. The sea churned like Vala's thoughts this morning. She knew she couldn't continue to battle the fates. Her destiny had been mapped many generations ago. It was up to her to prepare the accursed Norman.

Although she craved solitude, it was not to be. Within minutes, stones trickled down the path signaling the small footfalls of a regular visitor. Despite her warnings, the child Sibley had followed her to the cliffs.

"Tell me the story again, please," Sibley pleaded as she settled down beside Vala.

"You have heard it often."

"Please."

Vala smiled at the small face turned expectantly up to hers.

She sucked in a deep breath before she began. "Long ago, a people lived in Hafne. It was many ages ago. It was a time when Hafne knew nothing but love and peace. These people were called Ancients. Magical beings for they could do things that no normal man ever could."

"They had the sight," the child said excitedly. "Like me and you, Esma, Willa, Editha."

Vala laughed and stopped the child before she finished her litany of names. "The sight and so much more. They could see things, cause objects to move, appear out of nowhere and they did not die."

The child's eyes shone. "Magic," she said dreamily.

Vala continued, "It was a perfect world, the weather was warm, no wars, no hunger, nothing to cause them discomfort. Then one day—"

"The boats came," Sibley interrupted.

"Long before man walked on this island there were only the Ancients, then the Saxons came. They arrived in boats many, many years before the Normans. "

"There was a babe." Sibley peered seriously up at Vala. "A Saxon Ancient."

Vala smiled and ruffled her hair. "You know this story better than I."

"But I like it better when you tell it."

"That babe grew and became a woman, a gentle soul who had many of the powers of the Ancients yet different for she was half Saxon. She often spent time at the forbidden pond."

"Your pond."

"The Normans came one summer, long after the Saxons had settled this land. But one of the Normans was like none of the others, one with the sight that allowed him through the sacred circle that surrounded the pond. Eventually they fell in love and so the first child that held the blood of the three—Ancient, Norman,

Saxon—was born. It was a love match that created a girl child."

"She has never left."

"A ghost," Vala agreed. "She was killed."

"By her child." Sibley wrung her small hands together. "He was only a little older than me and very powerful."

"He was. But when the Ancients discovered what he had done they took his name."

"And then he cursed them. Because without his name..." Sibley breathed.

"He was mortal."

"Tell me about the curse."

"The curse," Vala said reflectively. "It has been upon this land for some time."

"Sibley!" Cecile's voice carried loud and brash through the early morning mist.

"Mother," Sibley gasped and her small face went white. She scrambled quickly to her feet and ran nimbly up the path.

Vala frowned as Cecile twisted the child's ear and dragged her toward the huts and out of sight.

Minutes after the child had disappeared small rocks again tumbled down the path and were followed by the subtle crunch of rock underfoot.

Vala glanced up but was blinded by a ray of sunlight. She squinted and shielded her eyes with her hand, and saw the outline of a man, Giles. She slid the dagger back into the folds of her tunic.

"An interesting tale. I expect you left much out," he said, as if she were his already.

She wasn't ready, not for him or for their shared destiny. She wanted to shout the words.

"Not many will brave that path," she said instead.

"You did."

Small stones rattled and skittered around him as he slid down. In a fluid motion he folded his long limbs and sat down beside her. He drew his knees up and rested his chin on his knees.

"What is this talk of a curse? The villagers seem much afeared of it."

"I thought you had no interest in hocus pocus?" She smiled quietly.

"Woman, you do your best to anger me. Yet…" His knuckle slid gently along her throat. He dropped a whisper light kiss on her forehead. "I would much rather do this." He cupped her chin and kissed her long and deep. The kiss spun into a different world, a world where nothing existed except the two of them. Vala sighed into the kiss, lost in him. For the scent of him was forbidden ambrosia, wind tossed pine and blatantly, totally male. And the feel of his lips, the taste of him was a temptation she couldn't deny. Her tongue dueled with his as her body began to throb and ask for so much more.

When he released her she could only breathe softly, her eyes locked to his. She wanted to fall into his arms and finish what the kiss had promised. She breathed in deeply and pulled her eyes from him.

"T'was spoken a long time ago," she said as she fought for reality and returned to his question. And even to her ears, the words were breathy.

"The curse? And the Rogue?"

"He is not a man."

"Ah, magic. I believe naught of that."

"That he is not a man or in magic?"

"Mayhap both." Giles put his hands behind him and leaned back. "Magna. Who is she?"

"Like a mother to me." She dodged the question. He would believe in his own time.

"This place will prosper. I vow that because I know that once it did." He sat up straight and looked out to sea.

She jerked. For he came too close to the truth, to the wealth that had once been Hafne.

"Everywhere I see fear and discontent. The old women glare at us from the safety of their cooking pots and the one child I have yet to see hides when we approach. Why is that so?"

"A land dying but not for lack of rain." His tone was reflective.

Below, the surf pounded and the air warmed as the mist rose.

"There is much wrong with this place." He turned to look fully at her. "I would like to know why."

Still she did not answer.

"Begin with why the keep was barricaded." His voice was gentle yet no less a command.

"To keep the evil within the walls of the keep at least for a time."

Trust him!

Magna's voice was a tad strident this morning.

"It was barricaded to keep the Others out and to make the villagers feel less afraid."

"The others?"

"Those that roam the woods and take the livestock."

"Ahh." He nodded. "Who are these ones that have taken my people's livestock? Tell me and I'll run them to ground before the day is out."

Vala sucked in a deep breath. Never in all her days had someone jumped to the defense of her and those she loved so quickly. She would have loved to name names and show him where they lived but she couldn't. She only knew that they existed, in premonitions and intuitive flashes, and because many of the villagers had known them.

"Once, before my mother and I arrived here to this place, men lived in this village who were Norman and something not quite human."

"Ancient." It was not a question, only a quiet confirmation.

"Partially. That is why so many of the women are now alone. Those men left, called by an evil that was once both man and Ancient. They live deep in the forest. Though they still live, they are dead to all in the village including their wives and families. They feed on our fear and live off our livestock."

"Yet they continue to live. Why have they not been brought to justice?"

"We have no weapons and few people. And there is one, more fearsome than the others."

She trembled slightly and closed her eyes. Her eyelids fluttered when she felt the soft brush of his fingers on her cheek. It was a comforting feeling meant to reassure.

"There was nothing that could be done. We had no army, until now." Finally the trembling subsided yet his hand still stroked her cheek.

"These men will not be free to kill," his voice was soft and oddly comforting.

Despite that, she knew he was wrong. "Not you, nor your men, nor anything human can protect us."

He caressed her jaw. His thumb traced the outline of her lips. Combined with the warm sun and damp mist it became an intoxicating combination. For a moment she gave in to the bliss.

"You are so beautiful," he murmured with his lips only inches from hers.

His finger grazed her upper lip.

She sighed before pulling away.

"I want you," he said. "It is the same for you. Is it not?"

Not before Helios shall the two become one. There was an edge to Magna's tone.

"There never could be that between us.

"You mean you will not lie with me? Is that what you thought my question? Ahh, sweet Vala, for now I only want to get to know you a little better. Some day I'll need a wife. Mayhap …?" His words trailed and he glanced teasingly at her.

"No, never!" Vala was shocked. Surely that was not what Magna meant. Marry him? Never! "I am Saxon." She prayed the gods would forgive the lie.

He chuckled. "Have no fear. I was not serious. Although I could be convinced of a dalliance."

"Nay! You are Norman. Tis bad enough that you have taken my … the keep," she said lamely and even as the words left her lips, she wondered at them.

"Your keep?"

Vala did not know what had caused her to say that. The keep had never been hers, would never be. Small hairs on her arms lifted.

Some day you will live there but not with the Norman. The voice was thin, weak, sexless and unfamiliar.

Vala picked a stone from the cliff and twisted it between her hands.

"Who are you?" he asked.

Her gaze met his and she shivered as the force of his energy. She dropped the stone and stared out to sea.

"I, too, am chosen."

"For?"

"To bring peace to the land." She rolled the material of her tunic, worrying it between her fingers.

"How do you propose to do that? You, a mere woman."

She resisted the urge to smack him.

"I did not mean in battle." She smiled sweetly back at him.

"What do you mean?"

"I mean my destiny is like yours."

"Hardly. My only destiny was to create a kingdom from this miserable keep and mayhap even the misbegotten vill –" He cleared his throat.

"Villagers?" she finished. "Aye, they are difficult but not misbegotten. They are not as ignorant as you would like. They have seen what Normans wrought. They do not want to be anyone's slave, not like—"

"I have no need of slaves."

He is your destiny, Magna's satisfied voice whispered.

A feather touch, his lips across hers. And then as quickly, he released her.

"The moon turns in a short time."

Her head jerked up. Had she heard right?

"The moon?" she whispered.

"Much less than a fortnight. You do not have much time." A shadow flitted deep in his dark iron blue eyes.

Vala's hands trembled. A hank of hair fell across her face as her wimple slid from her head. She should have plaited her hair but there were so many more important issues she had had no time to think of hair.

"I am not the enemy." He reached for her.

She pushed away from him and the wimple landed in the rocks.

Lies.

Again, the thin unknown voice came from nowhere.

"Why do women insist on wearing such things?" He lifted the covering from the ground and held it out to her.

She reached for it flustered, her mind on the voice and her hair flying around her face in the breeze.

"Friends?" he chuckled.

"I'll consider a truce, but not more," Vala said fiercely.

"I am comforted that you offer that, considering your hate for Normans."

"I still hate … most Normans."

"But not me." He looked at her knowingly. "I think you want more than a truce. As do I."

"It can't be."

"Maybe it must be, as it was foretold," he said. "I do not know how but if I want the curse lifted from this land, I need you."

A soft breeze blew brushed her face and then there was nothing.

"What is it that roams the keep? I can only think what roams is also what has the villagers brought almost to tears at the thought of sleeping a night within the keep or even a hut in the bailey. What terrifies them?" This last he said so softly that it was almost an undertone of sound.

"I have chores to complete this day," she said shortly.

"Stay."

"I am sorry, Lord de Montford, I must go."

"Call me Giles."

His hard look swept across her and then with a nod he looked away.

She was released. Just like that, like she was no more than a minion in an army, his army. She bit back retaliatory words and scrambled up the path. She stopped only once to glance over her shoulder. He had not moved. Instead he sat facing the sea as if facing the line of an already approaching enemy.

•

"By the saints!" he muttered after she left. He slammed his open palm against the rock. No matter how much he tried to separate himself from the magic, it followed him, tripped him and tangled him within a web that was stickier than any spider had ever spun. Voices out of his past, voices he refused to acknowledge, voices he had largely forgotten murmured softly to him and begged him to remember.

He had spent his entire life ignoring the magic that had stolen his childhood. He lived in a world of men, of logic, and of intelligence. Only the sight that would not leave him and the stone, that was his to protect, were allowed in the world he created. Until he arrived here, to this place that had been his reality.

Now Vala was changing everything. A battle had begun unlike any other.

"Jesu!" he growled. He had no idea how one prepared for a

battle such as that. Worse, he did not know if he could win nor what would happen if he did not.

Chapter Ten

The next day the village was quiet. Vala hesitated at the entrance of her hut.

Gather the first piece of the parchment.

The voice was weak and trembled with effort for it belonged to an Ancient, one of the others, not Magna. The power was growing.

"You do not have much time alone." Magna's image was faint. "Go quickly."

"Vala," Giles called from just behind her.

"Where did you come from?" Vala asked. This was uncommonly strange. There had been no one there, she was sure of it. Mayhap he was more magical than even he knew. Was it possible?

He frowned and looked around. "What was that?"

"T'was nothing. Only the wind and Magna."

"You speak yet again of nonsense, woman." He held out his hand. "Come. I want to talk."

This time it was Vala who frowned. "Nay, there are things that must be done this day."

"Aye and speaking to you is one. Unless, of course, you would rather speak here." He looked around where some of the women were looking up from their discussion at the well and others watched avidly from their doorways. A slight man strode past them, then slowed down, turned around and waited as if what was about to be said might be of great import.

Vala sighed. She couldn't help what she said next. "I suppose the parchment can wait."

"Parchment? There are recorded words here?"

"A story, aye."

"Excellent. We'll tell the story tonight, in the hall. What say you?"

Vala laughed. "It's not that kind of parchment. Tis magic."

"Enough," he growled. "Come." And he lead her from the village where many disappointed ears returned reluctantly to their tasks.

She let him lead for her curiosity was stronger than any resistance she might consider.

He stopped just outside the village beneath an ancient tree whose leaves drooped over the clearing and cast silver dotted shadows across the grass. "They respect you, the villagers. Do they not?"

"What are you asking?"

He let go of her hands. "There are so many questions of this village, these people. But I sense those answers will be revealed in time."

"You sense right, my lord."

"Giles." His hand skimmed lightly along her cheek. "So soft, yet so courageous. Who are you, Vala?"

"I am no different than the other women."

"And yet you are. To them." His breath fanned her cheek in a warm, intimate caress. "And to I."

"You?"

"Aye."

Tentatively she skimmed a thumb along his lip. Was it her imagination or did his flesh tremble beneath her touch? She moved closer. "There is something we both share."

He chuckled and his arms slipped around her waist. "There is much I would like to share with you sweet Vala."

"Aye. But there are many truths you must accept before that may happen."

"So it is the same for you too?" He drew her closer to him so she was pressed against him. She clung to him as heat flooded her and desire rushed through her hot and wanting. She wanted him here and now. Prophesy or not. Destined or not. She wanted him now.

"We both lead," she said.

"There can only be one leader." His kiss was hard and demanding. "Tis my keep. I shall lead."

"You have much to learn." She rose on tiptoes and kissed him softly. "I, too, lead."

"The women. For now." He lifted a strand of her hair that had yet again escaped her wimple. "I have learned that these last few days. You are much respected."

"We are both chosen. We have a shared destiny."

His grip loosened and he let her go. He took a step back. "That is nonsense. In the end there will only one leader."

She knotted her hands together and brought her thoughts back from earthy desire to where it should have been all along.

A chuckle wove through the clearing.

"What was that?" His hand went to his dagger.

"You heard it?"

"Aye."

"Then that is a start. That was part of the magic of Hafne."

"Enough." He waved his hand through the air as if brushing her off. "Enough. There is no magic. Belief in such only destroys." And with that he marched away leaving her alone and more confused than she had been in a very long time.

What magic destroyed what you held dear, Giles? she thought as she walked back to the village. In the distance she could see Giles heading back to the keep. To his reality, and she knew, to hide from the magic and the reality that was Hafne.

Five minutes later she found Esma at the edge of the village. Esma's thoughts were clear to Vala today. Esma was thinking of the Normans and all those that had come before, of the future and if there would be a future for Hafne. The thoughts slammed into Vala, one by one like rocks skipped over a still pond.

Vala bent close to her and whispered, "Do you still have the parchment?"

"Of course. I have not touched it since, since that time when - " Esma's voice trailed off.

"When my mother died. You can say it, Esma."

Fear flitted across Esma's features. "You think it is time to read it?" Her voice came out in a small whimper.

"Is anyone at your hut now?"

"Nay. Come." Esma grasped her elbow as they quickly made their way through the village.

Come to me.

The voice, feeble but poignant called to something deep in her soul.

"Vala, what is wrong?"

You are all I have.

Vala turned in the direction of the keep. "Do you see that?" she breathed.

"What?"

"A third tower."

"There are only two." Esma turned to look in the direction Vala pointed. "I see nothing."

"I must have imagined it." Although even as she said it, Vala knew she had not. The tower had been clear though faint, as it rose over the backdrop of the keep.

"It was nothing," she said and looked away as she walked faster. The hut Esma shared with her widowed mother was just to the right of the village well. Single file they ducked beneath the doorway into the meager light of the fire that danced over the hearth.

Esma knelt in front of the hearth and began to dig with her eating dagger.

Vala pulled her dagger from her belt.

Esma continued to scratch where the dirt had settled around what had been buried only seven short years ago. It was one half of a parchment the other half had been hidden by the Ancients at a place known only to them. But both must be joined before the time of Helios when the moon passed across the sun.

Vala bent down to help her. Finally the leather packet broke free. Vala reached for it and untied the thong. The leather fell open as Vala dropped it with a gasp.

Esma leaned forward. Her eyes lifted to meet Vala's. "Part of it was taken," she whispered.

"There are now more than two," Vala whispered back as if the very walls were listening. She stared at the fragile parchment before her. It was torn at the bottom as expected. But part of the other half was singed and clearly burned off. This piece of parchment was neither the beginning nor the end.

The parchment had been torn in two, one she had and one was in the keeping of the Ancients, yet now there were three or more. Where was the third? Vala swallowed softly replaying conversations with Magna and with her mother. She had buried one piece of two halves, and yet it was obvious someone or something had been here.

Gingerly Vala picked up the piece of parchment. Warmth tingled beneath her fingers.

Magna had told her as a child that the prophecy had been written long before the Year of Our Lord, before recorded time, during the time of the fabled Mervaine. Mervaine, the eldest of all the Ancients who had led them during the age of peace and who had offered them hope to break the curse the Rogue had spoken upon the land.

"What are you thinking?" Esma asked for Vala had retreated so deep within her thoughts that Esma couldn't reach them.

"What it would have been like before any of this, before the Normans came that first time. Before Mervaine disappeared."

"Vala," Esma hissed. "Do not speak of him."

"Or what? He'll return? We could well use his help."

"You will anger him."

"Name him, Esma. Name him! It is not Mervaine you fear. Tis the other." She drew in a breath. "The Rogue … It is our fear that makes him strong."

The walls breathed silently around them and whispers of rain splashed on the roof and ran down the outside wall. Within the hut, dry dust swirled in the air.

A glow rose from the dirt floor and spread through the ancient parchment. Vala bent forward and almost dropped the fragile piece as faint spirals of ink curled across the parchment. Light spiraled and settled on the delicate message. The words were clear as the voice of a stranger roamed through Vala's head.

Within the sacred truth of the pentagram.

Then the message became indecipherable although the strange letters carried on.

Vala shivered. The air tightened around her and she choked in the dry sharpness of it. Soon, very soon, she must unite the parchment and the two halves of seer's stone. It was then that she would face her destiny.

It would be days before she would realize how very wrong that thought was. Her destiny was so much more.

Chapter Eleven

The fire flared. A branch broke and popped. Vala propped her chin in her hand and stared into the flame. The runes lay spilled in front of her.

Willa bent over them, her brow furrowed. "I have never seen the runes so unclear."

Vala traced her finger in the dirt. "Anger, much anger," she murmured.

Then, as if by a trick of light, the runes changed.

Willa gasped. "Death!"

"We knew there would be more death before this was done," Vala said.

"I shall read them again in the morning." Willa gathered up the pieces of sacred wood and placed them in a pouch that hung from her waist.

Long after Willa was gone Vala stared into the fire. Finally, in the early morning hours after the fire had burned to embers, she went to her hut. Even then she couldn't sleep. Instead she pounded herbs with her pestle.

Only a few hours later pounding awakened her as the door shook in its frame. Then the door was flung open and Nelda's husband Edric stood in the entrance. "I'm sorry to awaken you but it is Nelda. Her time is here."

Vala wiped sleep from her eyes. "Go back to Nelda. I'll only be a few minutes."

The door thudded in his wake. Vala sighed. It was a bad omen. If these were truly birthing pains it was far too soon for the babe to live.

Only moments later Vala arrived at Nelda and Edric's hut. She tapped lightly and entered. Edric glanced up and relief was etched on his face.

Vala gently urged Edric away. The babe had already crowned. There was nothing she could do for the babe but ease him from his mother. With sure hands she held the small babe cradled in her arm while with her other she removed the cord from around its tiny neck.

Nelda's harsh breathing marked the passage of time as Vala worked. Edric's tension shimmered in the little room while Nelda's ragged breaths urged Vala to make everything right.

The sun streaked through the cracks in the hut, lighting the look of hope on both Edric's and Nelda's face.

"Is it a girl?" Edric and Nelda both asked hopefully.

Vala brushed a tear, for she knew why they asked. A girl might live.

Tenderly she drew a cloth along the babe's tiny limbs. She glanced up and saw that Edric wiped his wife's forehead with a cool cloth. Vala kept her back to the couple as she cared for the tiny babe.

The child was blue. But Vala was unable to speak that truth to Edric or Nelda. Instead she finally said, "It is a boy." In truth, she still hoped for a miracle. For the parents were but Saxon. The boy babes, those with Norman blood, began to die that year in 1065. The year the curse had begun. Since then it only got worse. She pushed her fingers against his small chest, an instinctive action that came from knowledge deep within her. Still, there was nothing. She scooped thick mucus from his small mouth.

The gods already wait for him.

Magna's words swept over Vala.

"A boy, Edric," Nelda said softly. There was a slight tremor to her voice.

Vala placed the small body carefully on the blanket and rose.

Edric looked sharply at Vala and then spoke to his wife. He whispered to her and stroked her hair.

"Our babe is dead," Nelda whispered.

"No!" Edric roared. "Let me see my son."

Vala placed the small bundle into his father's arms. Edric pulled the blanket back from the tiny face and stroked his cheek gently. Then he passed the babe back to Vala.

He stopped by the end of his wife's pallet and reached down.

"No Edric!" Vala cried.

"Hush woman, you have done enough."

Vala grasped his arm but he tore free. She followed him outside and watched helplessly as he threw the basket containing the afterbirth to the ground outside the hut. If the child had lived, the basket would have been burned to signal the start of a new life. Instead, the bloody remains lay spattered across the dirt.

Edric stalked away.

After cleaning Nelda and straightening the little hut, Vala gathered her things and left. Over one arm was her basket for birthing and in the other arm was tucked the blanket holding the babe.

"The child was not meant to be," Magna said as she appeared at Vala's side. "There was nothing anyone could do."

"Like Rosaline's."

"That babe was planned but not destined. The stars fated that birth."

"The father Norman, the mother Saxon and Ancient both, and the babe male. I miss her. She was courageous," Vala said wistfully. "A Norman Saxon Ancient male and female will end this. That is why the Norman can't be the one. He is only Norman." She stopped and looked at Magna. "Why then am I drawn to him? And why do I feel you are right, that he is the one?"

"The prophecy is about more than bloodlines. And he is much more than you think."

Vala nodded. "And the full truth is still unknown."

"Hidden within the knowledge of the Ancients and the writing of the parchment," Magna said and laid a hand over the top of her staff. "Soon, child, soon you will know."

In the distance the sky was beginning to contort with darkening clouds. And just behind them, the afterbirth lay forgotten in a dark ominous slick on the ground.

The full moon was now less than two weeks away. A shiver caught and tangled at the base of Vala's spine.

•

Editha hailed Vala, her tunic flapping as she ran. Vala waited and cradled the bundle in her arms. In the rites of the Ancients, the babe must be buried before sunset. Her soul wept as she clutched the still bundle tightly to her chest.

"The boy's father?"

"He has not returned."

Editha frowned at this news but there was no time for further questions. She gently lifted the still form from Vala's arms. "Go, get Nelda."

There had been no boy born in Hafne since Wulfgar had betrayed them. For unlike many in Hafne, Editha knew what had happened. Vala was not the only one. Editha had been there too. She had seen the Rogue's return to Hafne. The year had been 1065 and it was the third betrayal. She knew them all like she knew the litany she prayed to the gods each night. The Ancient Saxon woman was raped and the child that resulted was the hope of Hafne until he killed his mother. And then there was Wulfgar who had betrayed them all and that was when the land had begun to shrivel and die.

·

In a late afternoon dusk, the women gathered. Freshly dug beneath the canopy of the Trees of Truth, the grave awaited the babe. High up in those same trees, unseen by human eyes, a Grechner bird watched, his olive green eyes clouded, his elegant blood-red beak lowered in respect for the small life preparing for its journey to the gods.

Editha again made the sign of the cross over the still form followed by the sign of truth, five points on a star, the pentagram.

Vala's thoughts were disjointed. There had been too much death these last few days—first Rosaline and her child and now Nelda's child.

Behind her Nelda let out a choked sob and then silently crumpled to the ground. Vala hurried away from the fresh grave and went to Nelda. She wrapped her arms around the shaking woman's shoulders.

Nelda's shoulders quivered but her sobs were silent. While Nelda fought with her emotions Vala's thoughts veered to the child's father. What did the man's absence and that of the few village men mean?

She drew her mind back to the present as Editha drew the veil over the child's face. The veil fell lightly over the babe with gossamer threads so pale they shimmered in the late afternoon light.

Magna appeared beside the grave. Her staff rose high to the

heavens. Overhead the clouds cracked open and shafts of light descended. Her staff sparked into the sky and Magna began to chant. She held her arms out to Vala and the babe was placed into them. The staff twisted in her hand and turned red. The Grechner shrieked and the human mourners collectively shivered.

Magna knelt before the newly dug grave. Gently she placed the child within and arranged the veil, pulling it back from the child's face. She stood, stepped back and stretched her staff horizontal over the grave. Thunder belted and a shaft of lightning answered the rush of fire that shot from her staff.

"He has returned to those that created him." And with that Magna vanished.

The thuds of dirt filling the grave were masked as overhead thunder cracked and lightning forked across the sky, but there was no hint of rain. Vala's eyes followed Nelda as she was led away clinging heavily to Editha.

The grave was barely covered when Esma was pulling at her sleeve. Her eyes were wild in the wake of what could only be a vision. "Come, quickly. They are trying to storm the keep."

"Storm the keep. They? Who?" But as she asked the question Vala knew.

"The men. Edric leads them."

"He sees nothing but the blood of his child," Vala said.

"And it is the fault of the Norman, so he says and he blames—" Esma stopped as if she had said too much.

"He blames me," Vala said softly.

They ran. And when they arrived at the entrance of the keep, the gates were closed. The village men crowded in front of them.

Two ran at the gates with hoes. Others hurled stones while Edric, Nelda's husband, bellowed for the Norman to appear.

The anger in the air was not good. It only added to the evil, to the power of the third tower and what resided there. Vala dropped Esma's hand. "Do not come any farther. It isn't safe."

"And it is for you? I will not leave you." Esma followed behind her and after Vala and Esma trailed Editha and many of the other women.

Between the rumbles of thunder, if one listened closely, were cackles. It was not just the women that followed Vala. The Ancients too followed and watched, for what happened here would affect them all.

The gates began to creak open. She glanced around looking for Edric.

"Edric!" Vala screeched his name above the roar of the Saxons' rage and the answering outrage of the approaching Normans. Ahead, the men parted and Edric elbowed his way through.

"You!" he bellowed.

"Nelda needs you. Do not do this," Vala implored.

He grasped her arm and his face bent low to hers. Spittle flicked off her face as he roared, "if you had done your job, woman, my son would have lived."

"Then it was I, Edric. Wholly my fault, leave the Norman out of it."

"The Norman! You side with the bloody Norman."

Vala fought the urge to wipe the spittle from her face. Her aura hummed and spun as she stretched her abilities and pulled the anger from him. The rush of emotions that shot from him would have slammed her backward had she not been prepared. The voices, the strength of the anger that swirled within him, all of it called to her until her temples screamed in pain. Her vision blurred.

Chapter Twelve

They defied him.

Giles' stood in the entrance to his keep and faced his people. But it was in the face of their rage that his evaporated. He saw into their souls, the futile hope; the despair that led to this moment.

"My son is dead!" Edric shouted.

"Dead?" Giles stepped farther from the shelter of the gates. "Was he attacked?" He remembered Vala mentioning the fear of the woods and what roamed there.

"Attacked! He was but a babe like all the others. He is dead because of a Norman, because of the curse. Because of you!"

"Aye!" The men stomped and pounded their implements on the ground and shouted in unison.

"I don't understand." Giles held a calming hand up. "Explain."

"What good? My son is dead."

Giles lifted his hand high and from the second tower saw Royce nod. He watched as Royce signaled the archers to lower their weapons. Below the small crowd continued to roar mindless of the imminent danger they had been under.

"Cease this at once!" Giles roared.

"Move, Norman bastard," one yelled. "We'll end this now!"

"Stand aside cur, or die!" Edric raged.

Giles glanced behind him and saw the reason for the sudden increase in aggression. His men were backing him, prepared for battle and marching forward to flank him on either side.

"Halt," Giles addressed his men. "Put your weapons aside. They will not be used. They are my people. I'll defend them, not attack."

He walked from the shelter of the gates and the safe proximity of his men toward the villagers. He stopped only feet from them.

"Why did the babe die?" he asked.

"Edric's babe was stillborn. Our babes continue to die," one man said when Edric remained silent.

"Normans started the trouble," another added.

"This land is ours!" Another dared. "Leave Norman!"

"Murderer!"

Giles rubbed his forehead. He could see Vala in the midst of the men. Her face was pale and she appeared disoriented. She swayed. "Vala!" he said sharply. He shouldered his way forward and the small crowd parted.

He reached her as she began to fall. Her body was weightless, safe in his arms. He could feel the delicate structure of her bones. Around him the silence was deep enough to choke. In battle this was foolhardy to be alone in the midst of the enemies' camp. He cradled her gently, his back to the men placing a barrier between them and Vala. For a second he considered that he had his back to the enemy. But they were not the enemy. They were his people.

They had widened their ranks and he was now in the center. He swung around. The women now joined the men. And again Giles was faced with how the women greatly outnumbered the men and how few men there were. He had no time to think on that fact. With Vala still in his arms he said, "I'll break the curse on this land. This I vow to you."

"How? It is not possible."

"We are doomed."

They spoke as if one.

Then Magna was beside him, her hand on his elbow as if she gave her support. Esma pushed her way through the crowd to stand on his other side. Editha was immediately behind her and so the ranks of women that flanked him grew. It was obvious who held the power, if he had not known it before, if the priest's feeble attempts to weaken it had not proven that. This show of support certainly did.

The men's demeanor began to change. Their weapons fell to their sides and the charged atmosphere slowly vanished.

Editha pushed in beside him. "Why has she not yet gained consciousness?"

Giles lowered Vala to the ground and then gently traced a thumb along her forehead. He knew his aura shimmered green and he knew when he heard the women gasp, what they had seen. It was one more of his long forgotten gifts. This place called to them all. Healer.

•

Vala.

Vala, her name whispered around her. The call of the Ancients for one that they thought of as their own. Her eyes rolled behind her eyelids as she slowly came to but the pressure of those too familiar arms did not change. He was still there, solid, holding her. Before all the others, he was holding her. It couldn't be borne, not now—not yet. Held by the Norman in front of Edric and the other men. It would only inflame them yet again.

She did not have the strength to take the pain of Edric's rage again, not today. She opened her eyes.

"We thought we had lost you." Editha's voice shook as she crouched down to whisper in Vala's ear. "Never have you been gone so long. Never. I was so afraid."

Editha clasped Vala's hands. "He brought you forth from the darkness." Her lip quivered. "We'll be forever indebted to the Norman for without you we are lost."

"And Edric?" Vala whispered. The man's rage had been so great at the loss of his child that she couldn't see him impressed by the Norman's ability to bring her back from the depths of a seer's sleep.

"You took their rage but the Norman gave them hope. Hope that the curse will end soon." Editha leaned close to Vala. "And it will. The time is upon us."

Giles reached down and without thought, Vala took his hand and was pulled to her feet.

"He speaks true," Editha spoke loudly to them all and the rumbles of agreement followed her words. "Sparks flew from the stone he carries."

"No more talk of stones, woman," Giles spoke firmly.

"Why not, my lord? There is magic in this world. Surely you know that. The good—" Editha glanced at him and then away to the burnt, hard fields, "and that that slowly kills."

"We'll bring this land to life by much hard work and naught else," Giles said firmly.

"Our huts are cold, dark. There is not enough wood," Cecile

said. "What are you going to do about that?"

"Why are you not collecting wood from the forests?" Giles frowned.

"Why, my lord? Are you daft? No sane man or woman, except she—" Cecile pointed at Vala. "Will go to the woods."

"If it were not for Vala, you and yours would have long sickened and died. You know that." Editha looked in danger of striking Cecile and may have done so had not Vala grasped her arm.

"What do you mean? Why will you not go into the forest?"

"It is cursed. No one enters the woods any longer. No one. It is unsafe." Cecile glared at Giles before switching her gaze to Vala.

"Seemed a peaceful place to me. There is firewood aplenty. And the pond appears more suited for bathing than the river." His frown deepened.

"The pond!" Shocked voices rose among the crowd.

"My lord." Esma said nervously. "Are you saying you have been there, the pond?

"Enough of this talk," he said. "I do not know what creature lurks within the forest but my men and I'll hunt it down. In the meantime we'll build pens for the livestock and I'll set guards to the forest edge."

"You, Edric." He motioned to the mourning father. "Take those men near you, gather your implements and I'll have some of my men meet you at the village gates within the hour. We'll begin work immediately."

No one moved.

"Go," he commanded and they went. They straggled from the keep's entrance, heading to their respective huts. The keep would be empty tonight except for his men. He did not correct them. Tomorrow would be soon enough.

•

Vala faced Giles. The air trembled, alive with the magic and the attraction.

"It is not just the two of us," Vala said urgently. "You must face your truth."

"Explain."

"You and I are chosen to break this curse," Vala whispered urgently. "No matter my doubts and whether I know the true reasons for it—it is true. Together we must try to end the curse before the next full moon.

"I do not know what you speak woman," Giles said as his memory flooded with similar warnings from long ago. As the old hag's voice lifted through the fog of repressed memory. Monti. The name emerged from a distant past and with a familiarity that made him stagger. He shook his head trying to dispel the memories and focused again on Vala.

"If I—we, fail, then many generations hence, another will be born and their turn will come. But it will be too late for those that live here now. I can't let that happen." Vala touched his hand. "Can you?" she asked softly.

"How do you know this?" he asked. "Why should I believe?" But he did. Every instinct in him screamed that she was telling the truth. His muscles flexed, the nerve endings tingling at readiness as they did before any battle. But this would be a battle like no other, one where he did not know the enemy, couldn't foresee either the future or the outcome. All he had was one woman, who he was hopelessly attracted to and an old woman who seemed to vanish at inopportune times.

"Good," Vala whispered. "Now at least you know who you do not battle."

Giles jerked as if he had been slapped. She was right. Only yesterday he had believed the battle was with Vala. In mere hours he had admitted that the battle had nothing to do with who would lead. It was so much more. But who was the enemy?

He reached inside his tunic and the stone sent a jolt through his hand. He withdrew his hand. Enough! The magic would end here, today. This was ridiculous. There was no curse, no destiny, no battles, and no magic.

He thought he heard a faint cackle at his elbow and glanced quickly down. It was nothing, only his imagination, confirmation that it must end. It had gotten out of hand.

•

The walk back to the village was brief and Vala took the opportunity of the few daylight hours to go back to the gravesite. To find peace where there was none.

Caught in her thoughts, Vala stayed longer than she had intended. It was late and the light had almost faded to nothing.

The wind gusted over the darkened earth, a gentle caress to the silent graves, confirming generations of history. Here lay the graves of all those who had gone before, her mother, Rosaline and the babes … so many babes. Behind her the forest filled with shadows that hid much. Vala folded her arms beneath her chest and slowly began to walk away, leaving the place of broken dreams.

•

"Fool," Ewaldo mumbled. Her body heat grazed him and his fingers trembled with the will it took to leave her, to let her walk away alive. Shivers roamed his body and the hatred brewed sharp and comforting. Beside him the brush rustled and a hare bolted into the forest. It stopped and its nose twitched in alarm.

A frightened mewl was broken by the rapid snap of the hare's neck. His long hooked tongue lapped eagerly at the warm blood that flooded across his hand.

"It won't be long now," he muttered and disappeared into the forest with his prize.

Chapter Thirteen

Giles sniffed the air as the aroma of roast pheasant temptingly filled the air. Editha had made good use of the pheasants he had hunted in the woods earlier in the day. His stomach rumbled. But it was late and the trestle tables were already cleared of the evening meal. He stepped over a hound lying amid scattered bones. In the hearth, smoke withered over a worn fire.

"Giles," Royce called and his words were slurred.

"Ale?" Turstin shouted.

Giles shook his head and turned toward the cooking hut. Maybe there was some food left that he could scavenge there. He stepped over another hound snoring amidst more bones. His stomach rumbled but nothing was left of the evening meal. He sated his hunger on a piece of stale bread he found hanging from the ceiling in a basket. He tore into the hard bread as frustration with the scanty meal and his troubled holding meshed with each tough, pulpy bite. The Saxons refused to remain within the keep unless he was there every moment to gainsay them. His men were aimless unless continually directed. He sighed. He couldn't blame them. This holding had not been easy for them either. Some, he knew were feeling much of the strangeness.

He strode from the hut. The night sky was black and starless. Giles did not take time to mull this fact. Instead he breathed in the night air in refreshing gulps. How was he to regain the control that was so quickly unraveling? His dreams of a home, of a great fiefdom were disappearing. He would not allow it. They would bend to his will, these Saxons and whatever else they were, they would obey him and no other.

Listen to the magic.

"No!"

Magna glided at his elbow. "Why not?"

"You know why?"

"Aye, I do." She glided in front of him and her staff softly lit the bailey with a shower of sparks. "Do you?"

"You speak in riddles woman."

"I do not. I ask only that you listen to what is inside of you. Admit who you are."

"No."

"Until you do, the women will not respect you."

"The men?"

"No consequence. Not here." Magna faded.

"Who led them before my arrival?"

"Remember the boy. Remember the stories. Many hours we have spoken. Remember."

He stood for a long time after Magna left and he didn't hear Vala until she was upon him.

"I have missed you this day." Her voice was soft in the darkness.

"Have you?"

"Aye, I have. The villagers have all returned to their homes but I told them that tomorrow they must see you here."

He faced her. "You have? Because?"

"Because that's what you want." She stared him down. "Don't push me, Giles."

"Don't push you, m'lady. You have a humorous streak. Do you naught?"

"Nay." She shook her head adamantly. "I have a practical streak. You need help and I am giving it." She pointed to the keep. "I stepped foot in there and from the looks of things you may need help with more than just the villagers."

"Enough!" he roared.

"You dare to speak like that to me. I think not, my misguided lord."

"Misguided." He was at a loss for words. She twisted everything around between her and her magic. "Come here." He reached for her and she danced away. Her slender body swiveled easily out of his reach. Her wimple this time was in her hand and her hair was braided. The braid swayed as she moved. It was like a languid dance. It was always thus when she was near. This time when he reached for her he caught her wrist.

"Mayhap, I need some help," he admitted as he reeled her in. She came easily enough, obviously no more intimidated by his bark than any of the villagers.

"Mayhap you do, my lord." She looked seriously up at him. "And mayhap I need yours."

"What can I do?"

"Believe."

"By the saints! Not twice in one night."

"Magna?"

"Aye. I don't know how much I can take. Tis wearing me down."

"Good. The sooner you believe, the sooner we can move forward." She looked at him seriously. "The sooner we can make this keep of yours prosper."

"Of that m'lady I can be in agreement. Lead on."

And it was that last command that he regretted as he followed and his eyes couldn't leave her as she walked with the elegant grace of a lady, a true lady.

She glanced behind and her look was all seduction. He was sure that pert wiggle of her backside was done on purpose. T'was not fair she should show some mercy.

"Where are you taking me?" And he hoped against hope that it was to her hut. Straw pallet and all, t'would not matter, the forest floor would do.

"We are going to see Editha."

"Excuse me?" he asked as she stopped and smiled flirtatiously.

"You thought otherwise, my lord?"

"Cease with that."

"What?"

"Giles. I am Giles."

"Giles." She began to walk again past each of the worn, flimsy huts until she stopped at one, no different from any of the other meager shelters.

"Editha," she called. "Tis me and," she paused. "Giles."

The door opened and the big woman leaned against the door. "Tisn't about the cooking is it and staying there?" She pointed to the keep.

"Nay, Editha. We'll straighten that out in the morn. Nay, I'd like you to put out the fire. Would you?" Vala asked.

A slow smile spread across Editha's face. She opened the door wider. "Come in."

Giles followed Vala inside where a fire danced in the hearth. "I don't see …"

"And that is exactly why we're here." Vala cut him off. "You must begin to see. Whatever has you fearful …"

"I am not fearful of anything."

"Shall I?" Editha asked from end of the room farthest from the fire.

Vala nodded.

Editha closed her eyes.

"Nay Giles, watch the hearth. See there is no one near it."

And as he watched, the fire died. The room pitched into shadows and Editha opened her eyes.

"A wind," Giles began.

Editha closed her eyes again, her face pinched.

"The hearth, watch the hearth," Vala reminded him.

And as he turned to the hearth, the fire built into a small blaze that gobbled up the largest log before settling into a comfortable flame. "You did that?" He swung to Editha. "Impossible."

The fire went out even as he saw her close her eyes and stayed that way. For long minutes he stared from her to the hearth and back again. Then she opened her eyes and the fire built to life once again.

"And you can't do this?" he asked Vala.

"Nay."

"Hmm," he replied.

"'Tis magic."

"Mayhap and mayhap not." He pulled her to him. "This however, I believe is magic." And he bent and kissed her.

Editha chuckled. "M'lord, I think you are beginning to grow on me. I shall be at the keep first thing."

"I shall look forward to it." He followed Vala outside into the evening air that was beginning to choke with cooking fires.

"There is much strange in this place. I can't say whether I believe or I do not. It is much to consider." He rubbed his forehead as if that would make everything more real.

"Tis. I have lived with it all my life."

"And I have avoided it."

"That is telling," Vala replied. "That you would avoid magic means that you knew of it. Perhaps someone close to you ..."

"Enough. The only magic I want to taste tonight is your lips beneath mine. Come." He crooked his finger.

And this time rather than resisting, she came to him for she too wanted nothing more this night than the magic of his kiss.

•

"The babes will continue to die," Vala said later that evening. It had been a day since the men had attempted their uprising and a day since she and Esma had retrieved the parchment.

"You have unearthed the parchment?" Magna asked.

"You know I have." Vala ran a finger along the edge of the rough board table. "It was one piece of three, possibly more." She glanced up at Magna but the old woman's back remained to her. "Where is the rest?"

"You did well, girl. The Rogue's power strengthens daily. Had the men been allowed to continue he would only have fed off the energy of their anger."

"I hid my mother's half of the parchment. I swore to her that it would be safe," Vala brushed shoulders with Magna so close was she, so anxious for answers. "What happened?" She eyed Magna. "I have always wondered about the other half, yet now there is a third, mayhap more."

"How did the priest obtain his power? Women have been in charge here from the beginning of time. Yet a man claiming to be a Christian priest had them cowering. Ask the questions and you will have your answers." Magna lifted the spoon and smelled the contents before putting the spoon back in the pot. "There are three, no more."

Magna dropped the spoon and bustled across the room. "Do you not remember what I taught you before you could even walk? Before your mother brought you to Hafne."

"How could I forget?"

"Since your mother left Wulfgar."

"To go to the Normans," Vala said bitterly. "And Wulfgar followed. Together they betrayed Hafne."

"Ahhh, child," Magna shook her head. "That was her destiny.

The curse once spoken must be."

Magna returned to churning the spoon within the pot hanging from chains over the hearth. She stirred with such vigor that the brew sloshed over the edges. "The women are not one."

"What do you mean?"

"I can't say. Just that with not everyone following the women, it was easy for the priest to take control these last few months. You know the rest." The pot disappeared and Magna stood alone before an empty hearth.

"Alfred found the parchment."

"No, he did not, nor was it any of the Others. But you're right, someone betrayed us."

"And you will not tell who."

Magna only smiled. "As they were foretold. The Norman. He is the key."

"The Norman knows nothing."

"Only yesterday you called him Giles. Only yesterday your desire was leading him slowly to the truth of the magic. Now you place false distance where there should be none. He is your destiny. Together you will fulfill the prophecy. But unlike you, he is unaware of his heritage. And like you, he is not totally without knowledge. Two halves make a whole – sometimes even three." She winked and the wooden spoon glowed in her hand. "Until the two are one, we shall be cursed. Yet nothing can happen before Helios when the moon slips over the sun. This I have told you before."

"I do not know what you mean."

"Do you not?"

Magna gave a smile more in irony than humor.

"There is little time. You are tied to the Norman."

But it was Magna's last words that destroyed any illusions that remained. "You belong together."

•

Again Giles's eyes roved over the pages of neatly penned records. Records that made no sense. "There are no numbers recorded here for the cost of grain." Giles thumbed the heavy parchment, and traced his finger along the ledger lines. "The numbers are out of order and there is no record of purchases over the last four years."

The keep's former steward hovered just behind him.

"Explain," Giles demanded.

"Ask her," the little man whispered feebly. "Ask Vala."

"Vala?"

"Aye, if it were not for her, he would not ..." the steward glanced furtively behind him before muttering anxiously. "He is here."

"Explain yourself. Who is here? And why would a mere woman interfere with the records?" Giles scratched the fresh stubble on his chin.

"If it were not for her, he would have killed us all," he said, looking more and more anxious. "The time is coming."

"What has that to do with the records?"

"The less he knew about us the safer we were. Vala hid everything until Wulfgar died. And then it was too late."

"God's tooth man, spill the name. Who is he? Name him."

"Nay m'lord. He has no name."

"I command you."

The little man shifted from one foot to the other. He twisted his hands together and began to shuffle backward and away from Giles. "Only, the Rogue," he muttered and fled.

Hocus pocus. That's what Vala had said when he had asked her. What truths lay within the web of lies? Gile shook his head. The steward made absolutely no sense. No one was named Rogue. That word was a condition of being, not a name. He went back to the records, yet his gut clenched and his instinct screamed that they hid something far worse than he could imagine.

Chapter Fourteen

The next day dread knotted in Vala's belly. The time was edging nearer.

Vala entered the hut and softly closed the door.

"Leave the parchment, I'll hide it here for a brief time. The stars do not align and words can't be whole. Soon though, for my time nears," Magna said.

"I wish it were not so. There is nothing I can do?"

"Nothing, child. You know that. You have always known that."

"I'll get the stone. Tell me where ..."

"No, child. It is too soon. Go to the crypt. Stay well away from the pentagram for now. Bring only your pure aura and leave with nothing else. You will feel the truth of your destiny."

Outside the air was no less oppressive and stank of too many cooking fires in too small a space. Vala looked up to the keep. A figure was silhouetted beneath the faint moonlight.

Giles. She bit back the urge to go to him. To wrap her arms around him and to tell him everything, to lean on those broad shoulders and ... Nay.

Darkness closed and from somewhere close by, a whisper rustled the dry grass.

The pentagram, you must—the remainder of the parchment rests there.

And it was thus that Vala thought she learned what she must accomplish this night. For now, there was nothing to do but wait.

•

Giles slammed the tankard down and ale sloshed over the sides. Why could he not bed her and forget her? Her kisses only tortured him. He lifted the tankard and took a healthy swig. He couldn't banish her from his mind. Christ's bones, he had considered taking her to wife. She was Saxon! A Saxon no matter how pretty was for labor and, if they were lucky, sport and not else. Nay, not Vala she would not labor not here, not ever.

He would not think of her. He forced his thoughts elsewhere. The rumble of noise in the hall was deafening. That alone should take his mind from thoughts of her.

He shoved the tankard down the table and rose to his feet. The feeling of being watched was inescapable. His hand moved to his sword but by the time he reached the pillar there was nothing, only a chill in the air and the scent of evil.

Death tainted the air. Giles felt the truth of it deep in his bones. A gift from his mother, this ability to sense and feel what others did not. And as a result he had been able to keep his men alive in overwhelming circumstances, earning him their unflinching loyalty, a legend among warriors, and eventually this keep.

There is much evil in this keep.

"Show yourself!" he commanded in a throaty whisper, not wanting to draw the attention of the others in the hall. Even in this alcove there were too many people near who would hear, who would not understand. God's tooth! He did not understand himself! He walked deeper into the alcove away from listening ears. He knew the moment that he was not alone.

Magna leaned against the wall. Her eyes twinkled like she was about to laugh. "The priest was not without support. There are others." The statement popped out in her usual cryptic style.

"Others?" Giles asked.

"Hidden in the woods where they plot and plan."

"Plan what?"

"They are the keepers of the curse."

"Curse?" Giles put the question out hoping more information would come from this creature.

"Look around you. The land, the people, this keep. You opened the keep. Now you are responsible."

"Responsible?"

"You gave strength to him by your presence. You must stop the evil."

Mist began to form around her feet and Giles knew that she was about to vanish.

Frustrated, he tried to detain her and reached out to grasp her arm. There was nothing, only a mist of warm air but still her face was clear before him.

"What are you?"

Ask Vala ... Your destiny.

Magna's voice wound around him although her image was gone.

Soon she'll need you.

◆

Within the unseen third tower, he stroked the edges of the burn mark that singed a jagged line and separated the parchment. Even now the words of Mervaine were clear. He stroked the scroll with a long finger. The parchment trembled under his fingers.

Longing swept over him. He closed his eyes. It had been so long since he had belonged and now the moment was so close. "I need you," he muttered. "Come home to me."

Again, he smoothed his finger along the parchment as the words, once so clear, faded.

He gritted his teeth. Soon they would all die. The people, those untrue, those who did not carry the blood of the three and those who did not bind to him, all would be gone. Even now they starved on dry land beneath rain-studded skies because of a curse he had spoken so long ago.

He rubbed his hands together and snarled, "Daughter." He shivered, the word delightful after all these years. "Daughter," he repeated and sucked in a quivering breath. "Vala."

◆

That night Vala crept along the cliff path at the rear of the palisade. The moon was silent behind a shadow of clouds. The darkness was complete except for the occasional flicker of the torch from the guard. She felt her way surely for she had been here many times as a child to enter the keep though a little known entrance. But where she was going now was the crypt that branched beyond.

On a fall night in 1065, Wulfgar and her mother had died here.

"It is a dark night for a walk."

Vala jumped and her hand flew to her mouth. She saw the too familiar shadow of Alfred in the darkness. "You are banished."

"You should have died as did the other whore," Alfred said. "Mating with that which was not hers. But her and her spawn are dead as they should be."

"Rosaline," Vala choked on the words. "She did not deserve to die."

"She thought she could end the prophecy. As if her love was the answer. Stupid whore." Alfred spat.

"She did not know that it was not hers to end," Vala whispered and choked, coughing softly in the darkness.

"That is why you will die," Alfred hissed. "You are too smart for a woman."

"Who goes there?" The deep bellow came from above them. A light flickered, showing the outline of a Norman soldier.

"Speak and you will die," Alfred hissed in a soft whisper.

"What did you hear?" Another voice joined the first.

"I thought I heard a woman's voice."

"You have been too long without."

A chuckle melted into the night air.

Alfred's heavy breaths were so close that Vala's skin crawled. She could smell the foul odor of stale sweat mixed with rancid food. She gagged and her breath came soft and quick.

"Rosaline was no threat to you," she whispered.

The clouds shifted and a warm moon glow cast across Alfred's face. He smirked. "She was weak. Only the strong will serve him in the end. It did not matter to me one way or the other if she lived or died. Although," he said thoughtfully, "her child had to die."

"How?" Vala forced the question, for as much as she wanted to know, she did not. "Are you killing them, the babes?"

"Oh, dear." His words were warm, gentle and so very deadly. "It is not I."

"But you know," Vala whispered.

He chuckled. "It is you."

"No!"

"Aye. You make your tonic beforehand. Do you not?"

Vala gasped and almost choked on the bitter rush of fear and dread. He was right. She did and then she stored it until it was needed. Anyone could have tampered with the contents at any time. "What was added?"

He shook his head. "Tell me what you have done with your piece of the parchment," he snarled instead.

"Nay!" She shook her head. "I'll see you rotted at the gates of

Hades first."

Light flickered behind the walls and a head appeared on the ramparts. A torch was held up and the shadowed face of one of the Normans looked down. Vala pushed tightly against the rough wood. She glanced to her right and could see the darker outline of the priest.

"You will tell me," he whispered. He took her arm and twisted roughly.

"Nay," Vala said and pulled free.

Vala felt with her foot in the darkness, concentrating on his words even as she nudged a large rock. She shifted slowly in the darkness.

"Ahh, your mother said the same, before she died."

Vala gasped as words eluded her.

"Your sainted mother was nothing but a whore. A useful whore," he purred, "but a whore, nonetheless."

"She followed her destiny." The words were true and surprised Vala.

"She followed her lover," Alfred snarled. "The one she splayed her legs for."

"Nay," Vala whispered.

"Tis true, whether you deny it or not. Look to your father if you do not believe me."

"You are evil." Vala shot back. "My father was not."

"Oh, you know so little." Alfred chuckled.

Vala eased back from him. "Then tell me," she whispered.

"If only I could, but I can't. The truth will not come from me."

Vala continued to move backward under the temporary darkness as the guards moved to the other side of the keep.

"Accept the truth. Act wisely and you may share in this keep's riches. They will not belong to the Norman for long."

"I don't know of what you speak. The keep was never to be mine." She squatted, hidden in the darkness. Her hand felt for the rock.

"The old woman was right? You know nothing?" His voice was filled with disbelief.

"Magna?"

She knew her destiny. Linked to the Ancients for all time but it was her ability to foresee things that was her heredity, not the moldy keep for which both Saxons and Normans had fought. A keep steeped in the scandals and battles of men with no ability to foresee the future.

A keep built by the Ancients.

Vala started at the sound of Magna's voice.

"You are stupider than most women I have had the misfortune to know."

"Just moments ago you praised my intelligence," she said softly.

"Even I can be wrong."

Vala's fingers brushed against something hard. The priest's attention was caught to the distant cliffs where the sea crashed angrily against the rocks.

She lifted the rock over her head and brought it down with all her might. The priest fell and lay still.

Overhead heavy foot falls became louder. Vala flattened herself against the wooden wall and held her breath. The steps began to move again, directly overhead. The light flickered and someone grunted and then belched. A light spray of spittle misted her cheek and Vala bit back the urge to gag. She wiped her cheek as above her steps drifted away and she could hear only distant voices. She moved away from the guards and the ramparts, toward the sea wall that backed the keep.

The parchment is within the pentagram. It was the only place. I am sorry my love. The voice was hushed, warm and full of love, so very like her mother.

"Maman," Vala said the Norman name without thinking.

As she reached the end of the path, it veered inward to the keep. The sea air was cold and harsh as it slammed against the rock-strewn path. Her hair whipped and slashed across her face. Then, the wind died as quickly as it had arisen.

The path turned downward to the sea and seemed to drop through rock. She reached a small level outcropping, her sight obliterated as the keep rose above the level of the land. Beside her and curving ahead was a huge boulder, sheltering her from anyone within the keep.

Vala knew that the boulder had a crevice just large enough to slide in. Waves smashed against the entrance. Vala waited for the water to pull back before slipping inside. As she ducked through the low narrow opening, water lapped around her ankles. Inside the tunnel deepened and she could straighten easily. The light punctured the darkness as the torch burned valiantly in the damp air, giving off more smoke than light. She lifted the torch from the cleft in the rock ledge while silently thanking Esma who was the keeper of this flame.

Within the flickering torchlight the first pentagram was marked in stones, five sacred points and within that was a circle. Vala lifted one of the outer stones.

Take the parchment for it is the only way.

Vala hesitated.

Quickly, break the pentagram. Enter the inner circle.

Still Vala did not move.

My only love.

Sexless. Poignant. The words trembled and called to her.

"Who are you?"

Your destiny.

Still Vala hesitated. She would not jeopardize the future of the women, of this land. She must be sure.

For the women!

The voice wove around Vala. Faint words echoed that sounded distinctly like "daughter." That could not be. She tried to focus but her thoughts were foggy. She moved toward the voice as with each step her will dissipitated. By the time she reached the pentagram she moved only to the sound of the voice.

Trance-like, she knew she must open the pentagram and move the stones. Once a break was created she ventured into the inner circle. Within the circle, she stumbled once over a small hollow before squatting down and instinctively beginning to dig. The dirt was packed but as she worked it became dry and soft and lifted easily away. She didn't know how long she dug.

Time spun and stopped.

The small metal box glinted in the torchlight as it broke free of the dirt.

Vala lifted the metal lid. She felt blindly and the crisp feel of very old parchment met her fumbling fingers.

Suddenly, the metal became icy cold, too cold to touch.

The box fell from her fingers and rolled into the darkness.

Whispers and scratches began to fill the dim space. Unintelligible sounds surrounded her.

The sounds increased and as she hurried to leave the pentagram, she tripped.

Metal scratched along rock.

She fell and her world went black.

•

Giles!

The voice was faint yet he was sure it was Vala. Somewhere deep in the keep she called to him.

Snores echoed in the hall. His hand curved into the pocket of his tunic and thumbed the smooth stone. His left hand reached for his sword and the reassurance of the hard steel against his hand. He pulled a torch from the wall. Immediately, a breeze dashed against his hand and the flame flattened. Then as quickly as it had almost died the torch flared back stronger.

The circle has been breached.

The air breathed silently around him and then it came again, whispers of sound building into a warning.

She is no longer safe from him.

Giles began to run as he followed only his unwavering instinct. She needed him and that alone took his breath away. He dove down the stairs, through the hall and toward the back of the keep.

The thin light of his torch flickered from one of the numerous drafts that squeezed through the breeches in the wood and stone. He slowed as he came upon a heavy wooden door. The same door his men had tried unsuccessfully to open only yesterday. It now hung open just enough so that Giles could see the moonlight streak lightly across the floor.

The smell of the sea assailed him. He stepped through the doorway and the wind slammed against him. He was in an open corridor. He glanced up, there had been a roof once but now that was gone and only timbers poked rough arms up into the night sky. There wasn't a star in sight, only the eerie glow of the moon.

Ahead loomed a wall, chinked stones with another heavy timber door. He glanced to the side and saw the wall of a cliff rising above him. Whatever this was, it was built into a cliff.

The heavy door, like the previous, was not closed. He pulled the worn leather strap. Heavy iron hinges screeched, then the door began to swing easily. A rush of damp air flooded around him. He continued forward amidst the rustles of the night scavengers and the chill of not knowing who was ahead.

A bulky shadow shifted only yards ahead of him. Then the vision meshed and blended into the darkness.

A scream rang, breaking the silence.

Vala.

He knew her voice with a certainty. He dropped his light. The torch flared against the dirt as it tumbled once, and then died. Giles moved forward but stumbled in the darkness. A pinpoint of light breached the black void and in that second, he saw him.

"Vala," Giles roared as he rushed forward his sword poised. "Vala, nay!"

Chapter Fifteen

Vala's head throbbed. Her side ached where she had landed against the rock. Pain shot through her body as she tried to sit up.

"Tell me where you have hidden the parchment," Alfred demanded. "The master needs all of it."

"Nay."

Alfred's features flared bright beneath the light of his torch. He held a rock over his head.

No one kills what is mine.

Again Vala heard the thin voice, nameless, yet oddly comforting. A shadow darkened the outline of the priest.

Vala choked and rot filled her nostrils. She shuddered as the form loomed larger. The room filled with the presence. The air became dense and sluggish as the being filled the space. Wings of cloth spread wide over Vala. A gentle fluttering filled her senses. She felt an uneasy peace. The shadow loomed even larger and more oblique before thickening around the priest.

Alfred turned. His scream echoed as the darkness settled around him. The air quivered. The darkness that had encompassed Alfred lightened as the rock fell from his hands and he crashed to the ground.

She caught his torch before it hit the ground.

"Vala!"

The voice was so very familiar and so very welcome. The hands that held her were strong and familiar.

Giles.

His hands swept the hair from her face. He cupped her face in his hands and peered closely at her.

She shivered and twisted from his grip. Something warm ran

down her arm.

Blood, she thought absently. The blood must have trickled over his fingers where he held her arm for he bent closer. She jerked away.

"God's teeth, woman, you're wounded. Sit for a moment. You took a hard knock to your head."

She sank down as her legs shook and threatened to fold beneath her. Dizzy, she clung to his arm before everything went completely black.

Vala felt a moment of panic as she opened her eyes to only the light of the torch vainly flickering in the choking blackness. A woman's voice whispered through the air and beneath it in an undertone was the deepness of a man's. Chills swept through Vala. A small groan escaped her and she slowly sat up. Firm fingers gripped her arm. She bit back a scream.

"Easy." The voice was deep and gentle. Giles. "The false priest will not hurt you. He is dead. I killed him."

She started as reality returned.

"Vala?"

"You?" Vala began and then thought otherwise. Let him believe he was the instrument of death for she couldn't name what had been here only moments before.

"The priest or whatever he was, Alfred. He is dead. The Ancients will deal with what remains."

Vala sucked in a startled breath. "Ancients," she breathed. "How do you know?"

"You want to talk of Ancients now?"

Vala waited. Even the whispers were absent now and the crash of the sea muted. It was as if everything waited for his answer.

He sighed heavily before speaking. "My mother told me stories of the Ancients when I was a child. I was fascinated by them until I grew older and realized they were only a tale—until I came here."

He held his hand out to her. "What do you hold?"

Vala's attention went to her lap. She had forgotten about the box. She had forgotten everything in the panic of the moment and the rush of relief that followed. The faint light illuminated the yellowed parchment. Carefully she opened her palm and the parchment, despite its age slowly, gently opened. She forgot everything in that moment until Giles' sharp intake of breath brought her back again to the present.

"The parchment."

"The second piece," she responded and did not ask him how he would know. Somehow in this place it seemed right. Like it was meant to be.

He leaned forward as he held the torch aloft.

"There is nothing." She tried to keep the disappointment from her voice.

"Nothing? There are all sort of strange markings. Another language I can't decipher it. Maybe more light would ..."

Again the whispers began to collect in the far corner of the room. Something foreign and frightening let loose a lonely howl and close to her Vala felt warm breath on her ear and Magna's voice.

Leave, child. The time is not right.

Vala grabbed Giles' hand, meaning only to force him from the bowels of the cave without long explanation. The voices gained in volume. He pulled back. She should have known that he would resist. He was a warrior after all, geared to making his own decisions in his own time.

"We must leave. While we still can," she urged.

The whispering and scraping grew louder.

The Tonic. You.

The words repeated over and over. To Vala the voice was familiar.

"I did not kill the babes," she whispered. "No! Lies!"

"Kill babes, you? Of what do you speak?" Giles whispered harshly.

Everything around them was silent as if waiting for what might happen next.

Giles held the torch to Vala's face. "What is this about? You are the birther and a healer."

"The priest said the poison was in my tonic."

"Vala, nay." Giles folded her into his arms.

His lips were on hers. Velvet soft skin against hers and she wanted more, she wanted all of him. She quivered and groaned against him.

Horror rode on the edges of seduction. Death and fear and arousal ignited her. His lips trailed along her neck, dropping to her chest, and she ached for his hand to move, to cup, to stroke, to stop the ache.

He pulled her closer with his free arm.

She let him.

She knew he couldn't stop.

She shifted knowing that if she encouraged him farther he would take her here, tonight. And she wanted that.

Your tonic killed.

"Nay." For her the spell was broken even as he rolled her nipple between his fingers, even as the arousal of rough material against sensitive skin warred and lost with the horror of words that came from nowhere and everywhere.

"Nay," she repeated.

"What?" He asked thickly but pushed her gently away. "You shout no in the midst of love making."

"Do you not hear?"

"Hear what?"

"Never mind. Hold me."

"I can't. I'll take you here. Is that what you want?"

A scream erupted from deep in the stone and curled around them. The air turned to ice.

"Come. We must leave," Vala pulled at his hand. "Now!"

"Close the circle," he muttered and as the last rock was put in place, a scream curled from somewhere nearby, only this time louder and so very familiar.

"This way." She grabbed his hand and began to move toward the passage from the sea and away from the tunnel that led to the keep.

Finally outside they both took in relieved breaths.

"Can you tell me all?" he asked. "Surely, after rescuing you from this I deserve the full tale."

"Not all," Vala said softly. "But you deserve some of the story at least, what I know. All is known once the parchment is together. Yet still we are missing one piece."

"The whole story and the complete parchment I will have before the full moon strikes again. I want peace here," he said simply. "As soon as possible. The full moon is less than a fortnight away. That should be ample time."

Then the world seemed to spin at a crazy angle as he wavered and said, "the burial circle must open." His voice was dreamy, as if in someone else's control.

"Giles." She thought to shake him. He was under a spell. Whose she was unsure. "Giles!"

His face cleared and he looked at her, bemused.

"What did you see?"

"I can't explain it," he said. "I saw a crypt. Who is buried there?"

"I do not know." She grabbed his hand. "No more questions. Not now. We must quit this place."

Below the sea roared, sending seething shards high into the dark sky.

"Why are you alone here? Where is your family?" He asked when the entrance to the passage was out of sight.

"They are dead."

"Dead?"

"Aye, my mother died these few years past."

"Who was your father?"

Vala jerked away. She was silent, her gaze distant before she spoke.

"I never knew my father," she said and couldn't stop her voice from shaking. "It is said that he died when I was still a babe. My mother never spoke much of him. When I asked, she would always tell me, another time." She paused. "That time never came."

She walked away, following the path, back to the village, away from him and to what had once been safety.

For Giles, there was no sleep to be garnered that night. Instead Vala's last words echoed over and over. Words that had rocked everything that he had come to believe about this keep ... words that changed everything: *My father was Norman.*

Chapter Sixteen

"Giles."

Vala's voice was sweet in the morning air but to Giles everything about her except for the mystery that surrounded her was sweetly enchanting. Still he shuddered. It had been a long night and now her nearness only brought those disturbing words to the forefront.

My father was Norman.

She caught up to him and took his arm. "What's wrong?"

He stopped and looked down at her. Her face was fresh and clean, her hair still wet. She had obviously been to the pond. He reached out and gently ran a finger down the damp, fine locks.

"Explain that your father was Norman," he said it bluntly only because it was at the forefront of his mind.

She took a step backward and he wasn't sure but there was something frightened almost like panic in her eyes. He wrapped an arm around her waist and tried to draw her to him. She drew away.

"I should not have said that." The words seemed to tremble on her lips.

"Why?"

"It is all I know. What Magna has told me. He was Norman and I know not else."

"Tis a Saxon village."

"Not really."

This time when he reached to caress her cheek, she allowed it.

"Tell me more."

"I can't. You must face who you are before you are ready for the truth." She took his hand between both of hers and gently stroked his palm. "What do you remember?"

He wasn't sure if it was the feel of her gentle caress against his palm, her nearness or just that it was time but he remembered.

It was a flood of memories, not just the bits Giles had remembered all his life, and it was so real he thought he might drown in it.

Legends and stories told to a small boy about an ancient stone of prophecy, a seer's stone split for all time.

You are the first male to carry the seer's stone. These had been his mother's last words to him, or had that been Magna. Giles was no longer sure. His boyhood was a confused mire of memories. The magic his mother had taught him was no longer part of who he was. It was the magic that he had denied when she deserted him. Magic reminded him of his mother. Magic had no part in a warrior's life, no part in the building of this holding. Magic, like his mother, was gone.

Memories long buried continued to flash through his mind. Magna had been there. She had been different. Not the aged creature that appeared so often now. Now it was as if the vitality, the energy that was her life was slowly leaving this plane.

Vala's destiny must be yours.

The voice was achingly familiar, a voice that had sung lullabies to him as a child. It couldn't be. His mother was gone, many years past and she was only a woman who had left her small son to fend for himself. There was nothing honorable in that.

His mind went back to the tale. The tale that said that a Norman, Saxon, Ancient woman held the second half of the seer's stone.

"Giles." Vala's voice was soft and full of concern. Her hands were a warm caress against his. And yet he couldn't share these memories for they couldn't be true. It was all too much. He pulled his hand free.

"Giles?"

"No Vala. Please. I need solitude." And he looked away from her as he saw the hurt and puzzlement on her face.

"Aye." She nodded.

And it was all he could do not to take that extra step to gather her in his arms. Instead he watched her walk away. As she disappeared from view, he yanked the stone from his pouch. It lay cold in his hand.

Words spoken decades ago, a tale that had always seemed so real to him as a boy, so magical, especially with the cadence of his mother's musical voice. He wouldn't think of her, he hadn't in years and he wouldn't start now. Yet her voice would not be silenced.

The ring he kept safeguarded, which he refused to wear, was a duplicate of the one Vala wore.

The blood of the new race shall carry the stones and the rings into the next generation. Two women shall carry the legacy that is Hafne to all the generations that are to come.

He didn't know where the words came from or where he had first heard them but they were true. He knew that with a certainty. Hafne, the story went, was a land unlike any other. It was the haven of the Ancients. Hafne, a land of eternal life, magic and peace, and a land destined to be cursed. He froze. What had Vala said about this land and this keep? She couldn't mean Hafne! Only that this land was different. Yet his gut screamed that maybe, just maybe, there was a Hafne, and it was here.

His lips tightened as he entered the keep. The gift of the sight and healing was one thing, the ring and the seer's stone another but he would not stretch those beliefs any farther than what they already were. It was too dangerous.

◆

By mid morning Giles' mood had turned foul. He stormed through the bailey and people scattered.

Magna appeared at his side. He refused to acknowledge her.

"Halt, boy," she commanded.

"Boy?" despite his temper, he was amused. She was Ancient in more ways than one and harmless.

"Where is it?"

Giles pulled the stone from beneath his tunic. He stroked it absently. *She could command armies of men easily*, he thought as he obeyed her without hesitation.

"It was my mother's." Giles held the stone in the palm of his hand. Magna glanced at it and looked up at Giles. "She could foretell events and she was a healer."

"She was fair with lovely, pale, blonde hair." Her eyes took on a dreamy cast and her features smoothed into youthful beauty.

Giles fought for composure. Blonde. Saxon blonde. The truth dredged from the hidden bowels of his conscious.

"Say it!"

"I can't."

"You must."

The stone heated and purple shards leapt from its crystalline center. He would have dropped it if Magna had not taken it. She held it gently while it shimmered with angry color.

The One. Identify yourself.

The words rushed at him, driving into his ears, flooding his senses. His vision fogged.

"Say it."

"Saxon!" he roared and around him all activity ceased and was replaced by the curious whispers of both Saxon and Norman as they worked together within the bailey. He glanced over his shoulder sending a look that would bode ill to anyone who did not return to his duties. He let the look trail a minute longer before he swung back to Magna.

"Saxon," he said in a much quieter voice as around him the natural rhythm of life in the keep returned in a steady hum. "She was Saxon," he repeated once again and felt the closest thing to defeat he had ever felt in his adult life. He closed his eyes.

He opened his eyes when Magna took his wrists. Heat flooded and raced through his body from where she touched. It was a heat that carried knowledge, truth and trust. He was drawn deep into her eyes, into her world, into the truth.

"She could foresee and sense what others can't. Like you."

Giles nodded. His world was tipping on its well-organized edge. And as suddenly as these thoughts raced through his mind, the strange event was over. It was like nothing had occurred. There was naught but an old woman standing before him. Yet everything had changed. Magna placed the stone in his hand.

"It is not the only one."

"I know of other healers with such stones." Giles tried to steer the conversation to some level of reality.

"Not like this. There are two. They must be joined. You must watch for the signs," she paused and stared into the sky. "Watch the sun. That will be the first sign that the time is close."

"What do you mean?"

"The curse can be broken."

"Tell me," he commanded with the frustration of knowing she would not. "Why must you speak in riddles?"

Magna continued as if he had not spoken. "It was not meant to be alone. The evil will not leave until you are united."

"Why will you not tell me? I want what's best for the keep…" he paused, "and its people."

"When that is true, you will have the answer," Magna answered sagely.

"Woman, you try me," he said and then realizing that she would not give him a full answer he asked, "What do you know of the ring Vala wears?" Vala's ring was almost identical to the one that his mother had worn. The ring had come down from his mother's line.

"I gave the same ring to you when you were just a pup." Magna's expression was melancholy. "You were such a sweet boy. I had high hopes for you."

Giles started. The witch had read his mind. She knew of his ring.

"Of course, boy. You have yet to learn to hide your thoughts."

Giles shook his head. He could only stare at the little woman and ask, "Ye gave me the ring?"

"Someone had to. Your mother was gone."

Magna rapped her weathered and twisted staff sharply on the hard ground. "The first male to wear the ring. It is also your identity. Beware. Evil is drawn to it for that is its purpose."

Magna moved away from him. "Do not wear the ring yet for it is too soon for you." Then she disappeared behind the cotter's wagon where a puff of mist was the last he saw of her.

"Identity, Jesu!" Giles rubbed the back of his neck which for an inexplicable reason was beginning to ache. "Whose identity?"

The whisper seemed to skim amidst the breeze that traced suddenly through the yard and wrapped around him before skittering away. It was a voice that was neither male nor female.

You are the one.

Chapter Seventeen

The next day, Giles left the keep early. He needed time alone, time to think, away from the bustle and flurry of activities that heralded each new day.

He couldn't make sense of much of what Magna had said nor what had happened in the cave last eve with Vala.

It was only a short ride to the pond and Ramion relished the exercise. He had been cooped up too long. They both had. At the pond Giles had expected that Vala would be there and despite a craving for solitude he was disappointed that she wasn't.

He left the horse and began a slow exploration of the clearing. He had seen little of what surrounded the village and the keep. He hadn't much time with everything that had happened in the short time since he'd been here.

Hafne, he shook his head.

Hafne, a woman's voice echoed.

"God's tooth, don't mock me! Show yourself." His gaze traveled over the clearing. The giant lime green leafed trees that reached for the heavens were silent. The still turquoise pond, surrounded by lush grass and brilliant flowers such as he had never seen gave no answers. Nothing moved. His eyes were drawn into the treetops again where a hint of olive distinct from the brilliant lime of the trees seemed to be looking at him.

"You are losing your mind, de Montford. There is nothing watching you in branches so high a mere man could never reach."

Do not be blinded by man's reality. There is so much more.

The pond shimmered. Waves lapped the shore. A red glow seemed to churn just below the surface of the water. Giles glanced up and saw the red was a reflection of the long beaks of six birds that clustered high in the trees. The birds towered over the tops of the trees for they were the size of a good-sized child. Their long red beaks and olive green eyes watched him, unblinking.

"I have truly lost all sense," Giles muttered. He glanced over to Ramion who stood quietly with his eyes half closed in the morning sun, as if nothing untoward was happening around him. "Maybe this is not true." He shook his head. "Not real."

Mayhap.

The voice was no longer disembodied. It was clearly Magna. She was nowhere in sight.

"What do you want from me?" He roared.

"You must accept who you are," Magna's voice was soft and right at his elbow.

Giles swung around. She wasn't there. He was alone except for the birds whose presence was confirmed in the red glow that still warmed the pond.

"I am Giles de Montford!" he bellowed.

"And so much more."

This time Magna's voice came from high up within the treetops. Giles glanced up and saw the eyes had disappeared and the color of the leaves had turned from lime green to solid red. The entire clearing was bathed in red.

"Blood," Magna said sadly as she appeared in front of him. "Hafne's blood."

"What are you trying to tell me old woman?"

"You must admit who you are. You must do it soon."

"You are sorely trying my patience."

"I expected so much more of you, Monti."

"What did you call me?"

But he was alone. Other than the strange virulent green foliage, nothing was different here than in any other part of the country. Nothing, he told himself.

Monti.

Despite all his warrior logic, memories flooded back with the strength of a storm tossed wave. Affectionate words, the pet name the old hag had bestowed on him. Magna, she had been his childhood teacher for such a short, magical time. It had not been a dream. Giles sank to his knees and clasped his head in his hands.

Love. The wise old voice caressed his ear. *Love.*

And as if the words had conjured her up, she was there. At first there was only a brief movement, a shadow in the trees but it was her long blonde hair that gave her away. For it floated free on the breeze, lifting gently around a gauze gown she wore. Like what she had worn that day so many days ago when he had thought her but a wood nymph, it floated around her concealing and revealing in turns.

"Vala?"

"Aye," she said from the shelter of the woods. "Why are you here?"

"I would ask the same of you?" He pursed his lips. "Why do you hide? Come out," he commanded.

"'Tis the one place that gives me peace," she replied as she came to him on bare feet that seemed to float on the forest floor.

He reached for her and drew her softly into his arms. "I want you," he murmured softly against her neck.

She drew back. "Nay, Giles. 'Tis too soon."

He frowned. "Is that agreement of sorts?"

Her smile almost slayed him where he stood. It was that sweet. But her words were his undoing. "Mayhap, in time."

"Mayhap, today."

She crossed her arms across her chest.

So that was the way of it, he thought as she hid the shadow of her nipples from view. T'was not going to be like their last encounter in these woods. She ducked around him.

He stopped her with a hand on her arm. "Vala, wait."

"I'd like to get dressed."

He swallowed back a rush of disappointment that told him he would not be holding her in his arms again, not this day.

•

Thanks to the Ancients, soon Vala would be his. For because of one of them, the words of the verse of a long lost god had sung in the depths of the Rogue's mind through all the lonely years and centuries he had wandered the earth. The verse had allowed him to live. Because of the wisdom of those words, when his first physical form had begun to die, he had found another. So it had gone, century after century.

Less than two score years ago, he had found a man beautiful as only a powerful Saxon warrior can be. He found her, alone, and as beautiful as was he. When he took the woman, she too was ready, for it was the only way.

To find one such as Vala's mother outside Hafne was very rare. Away from the guidance of the Ancients she had been vulnerable, available, his. And now, even though he had only just learned of her existence, the blood of that union, Vala, was in Hafne where she belonged—an Ancient/Saxon/Norman with potential so powerful it even frightened him.

A cackle slipped from his lips, one so very similar to the Ancient's cackles, yet so very different. He rubbed his hands, chafing the skin in his glee.

Chapter Eighteen

Giles stood in the keep's entrance and was pleased to see that the bar had been replaced with fresh wood but immediately frowned as this thought was followed by a dank smell. The torches were out and only dim light skirted the edges of the hall. The windows were still covered with soot stained clothes to keep out the winter winds. The cloths had obviously hung there since the last occupants many years ago. This morning he had ordered Editha to have them removed.

Giles sighed and went in search of the woman. His boots trod hollowly in the great hall. At one trestle table a couple of men diced. Scattered around and under the trestle tables, the hounds slept snuggled in the filthy rushes. Women's voices came from upstairs. He began climbing the stairs as the voices became louder.

"You can't ignore his commands."

"Not all but some. We have been at the mercy of too many for too long."

He stopped with a boot on the riser. *An interesting comment,* he thought. Considering the keep had remained empty since the last Saxon lord had died. He waited for what was to be said next.

"There is nothing we can do."

"Not about him or the Others. But there is much we can do about the Norman."

"He does not need to be too comfortable."

A giggle followed that statement.

"Even though he is chosen, he'll soon learn who gives commands in Hafne."

Giles began to climb the stairs. If they would be men he would have bashed their thick skulls together. As he came into view he was greeted with the frightened face of a woman he couldn't name. Yet her face was familiar as one of those from the village. Another gasped and covered her mouth at the sight of him. A fourth woman backed quietly into the shadows. Only Editha faced him.

Giles held back a sigh. He had ordered the keep cleaned. The clutter and rubbish had been removed but still the rushes had not been changed nor had the cobwebs been swept from the rafters. The smell of burnt wood filtered easily down from the rafters. The wooden beams had not been replaced. He would have a word with the woodworker when he was finished. He met Editha's glare.

"Explain, woman. Why have you not followed my orders?"

"My lord." Editha shuffled toward him. She almost made him believe her submissive nature until he saw the challenge in her eyes that refused to look anywhere but directly at him.

"That is clean?" he asked shortly. He pointed at one of many cobwebs. It had been a difficult week and he had no patience left.

"I can't supervise everything. I was busy with the cooking."

"Editha!" The sharp voice caused both of them to turn.

He met blue eyes so deep that he thought he was going to drown. Vala stood before him with her hands on her hips and a determination that left no doubt that in this moment, she was warrior, a warrior that he only wanted to gather in his arms.

Instead she stepped around him. Editha tilted her head toward Vala while ignoring Giles. He gritted his teeth while Editha grabbed her broom and began to sweep as the other women scattered.

"I'll organize them and we'll get the keep cleaned." Vala glanced upward. "Edric did not replace the timbers?"

"You thought he would?"

"I suppose not. He needs time. He is mourning."

Giles looked up at the burned marks scattered across the beams. "Who did it?"

She hesitated.

"Tell me," he said softly.

"Will you believe," she asked and her finger traced a gentle trail along his forearm.

"Mayhap," he reluctantly admitted.

"The Rogue. After Wulfgar died, his excitement was intense."

"What more do you know of this?"

"I do not want to talk about his arrival again."

"And you shall not, once you have told it to me once."

"I can't, not here."

"Because this is where it began?"

"No." Her eyes met his, shock adding depth to the cobalt blue.

Immediately, Giles realized his error. He had not begun here. Rather at the crypt where the prophesy had begun. "Yet this is where He waits. Is it not?"

"He is not strong enough to go far."

"But soon will be?"

"Soon." Vala nodded her head.

"He awaits the change of the moon."

"And in the meantime the energy of the Others sustains him." Giles grasped her elbow and moved her to a far corner of the keep where they couldn't be overheard. "I do not understand how they sustain him but the others must be cut off. Slain before their rot spreads," he hissed.

Vala yanked free and ran outside. She confronted him in the bailey in a corner away from the activity by the outer walls and away from prying eyes. "You should not have said that, not there. Do not speak against him within those walls."

She grasped Giles' arm. He trailed a thumb along her cheek and fought the urge to kiss her.

"Listen to me." When she had his full attention she continued, "you must protect yourself. If he has heard, he'll seek your end."

Giles glanced toward the tower. "My life has been in danger before. This enemy may be unseen but not insurmountable."

The smell of onions was overpowering and Giles fought the urge to turn away. Mercifully, the noxious odor faded as Magna appeared.

"You are his most immediate threat," Magna said.

"What can I do?"

"Nothing. Continue on the path that was prophesized."

"Nothing!" His voice rose but of course, Magna was gone. "Now what?"

"We deal with the here and now. I must see to Editha and the others."

"I'll come with you. Mayhap, I'll learn some of your tricks," Giles said with a grin trying to lighten the situation.

"To making Editha obey?" Vala answered with a smile. "There

are none. Just long association and naught else."

"Ah, Vala, that is where you are wrong," Giles replied totally serious now. "The women respect you. That is a surety." He turned her to face him. "Sweet Vala."

"Tis not the time," she whispered. "Let me go."

And he did like his will had vanished and been replaced by hers. He took in a deep breath even as Vala tossed a hank of hair that dangled outside the confines of her wimple and hurried toward the keep.

Giles could do nothing but follow.

Vala stepped over a snoring dog. As she did, she reached down and chucked its chin. The dog snuffled and opened an eye and immediately rolled over on its back, begging to have its belly rubbed. Vala chuckled softly and complied. She was still chuckling as she rose to her feet.

He couldn't resist. He brushed a wisp of hair that floated across her forehead. His hand lifted the wimple, releasing some of her hair. Gently he traced the smooth skin of her cheek. Even as his eye traced the long line of hair whose pale beauty now flowed in a single strand down her chest, where the soft swell of her breasts gently lifted her tunic. "Would you giggle like that after a night in my bed?"

He couldn't believe it. She brought her foot down, obviously meaning to break every bone in his great toe.

In a split second he lifted her and slung her over his shoulder. His intentions weren't clear even to him. He only meant to teach her a lesson to take her outside away from the hearing of the others within the keep who he knew now avidly listened.

"Vala!" Editha shrieked. "Put her down you great oaf!"

The last thing he saw was the handle of the broom crashing across his head.

A lifetime passed before sounds filtered his consciousness.

"Ye killed him."

The words came through a deep fog.

"His head is too thick for that."

He recognized Editha's voice while trying to stifle a groan.

"It will be bad for all of us if you did."

Vala, sweet Vala, he thought.

Warmth caressed the side of his neck, then a light pressure

where his pulse beat strongly. A breeze chilled his neck.

"He'll live."

Vala's voice was as cold as the chill that had just swept over him.

He groaned.

"Can you hear us?"

Their faces slowly came into focus and he tried to sit up. Instead he was held down. He couldn't shake the strength of a mere woman. Frustrated, he groaned again. It was several moments before his strength returned and the room quit spinning.

He stared into the grinning face of Editha. "Enjoy it while you can," he snarled.

"Oh I will—my lord," she said with a chuckle.

Giles staggered to his feet, rubbing his head and called after her, "Ale, woman, bring me a tankard of ale."

Vala held out a foul smelling compress. "Put this on your forehead. It will ease the ache in your head."

He sat with the compress on his forehead. He could do naught else with his shaking legs. He frowned at another stab of pain. Before he knew it, she was back with powder.

"You would try to poison me?" he asked without conviction.

"Of course not. It is willow, nothing else. To relieve the pain."

"I have not heard of this remedy."

"Learned from the Ancients," Vala said shortly. "The Ancients have knowledge not known by others. Mix it with your ale."

He stared deep into her eyes. There was no guile, no deceit. The powder did not change the taste of the ale and he drank it back in one long pull. He wiped the ale from his mouth with the back of his hand and peered closely at her.

"You will sleep with me this night," he said, trying to redeem an ounce of male pride and a sliver of control. And even before she spoke he knew it was for naught.

"No." She picked up the empty tankard. "I will not."

"Aye," he muttered. "As you say, but only for this night."

"And many others, my foolish lord." She smiled sweetly at him and stroked his arm.

He reached for her.

She pulled away.

He tottered dizzily before grabbing the edge of a trestle table.

He glanced down. At least the woodworker had been busy at something. The table did not wobble as it had only days before.

"Remember, my lord, Giles," Vala whispered, her breath hot on his ear. "When that time comes, it shall be I who shall lead."

Giles sighed heavily and sank to the bench. Someone had refilled his tankard. He didn't remember Vala leaving to do it. His head spun and he took a deep breath. Why had he not seen it happen? He took a long draught of his ale before admitting that once again he had been bested.

The bench shifted as Editha sat down beside him.

"What do you want?" he growled.

"Despite what I say, we need you here. You were prophesized."

"What isn't?" Giles snapped.

"Seriously," Editha persisted, "it is written and both shall lead."

"Both?"

"Do you not listen? The women have power but only two shall lead. You have been told this many, many times," she spoke slowly like she was instructing Gilroy, the slowest of them all.

"Vala was born to lead." Editha held his gaze, silent, forceful, "as were you. That is all. The rest you must learn for I know naught else." She stood up. "Except," she smiled craftily, "for the power of three."

"Jesu," Giles muttered. Women, leaders within this, his fiefdom, maybe once in a land of their own making, but not here, not now, impossible. First there had been the magic, the curse and now this. Slowly his dream of an obedient wife tending hearth fires and listening docilely to his tales of long ago battles was falling into ashes like an untended fire.

Chapter Nineteen

Giles had been on his land for over a week. The palisade could now withstand the initial advances of any marauders but the mysteries that stonewalled him at every turn remained. For despite promising to tell him everything, Vala had continued to remain secretive.

That would end. It would end now, Giles thought as he stormed toward the village.

He returned to the hut of Magna and Vala. Without knocking, he pushed the worn wood door open. He fully expected the hut to be vacant as it had been before. Instead, a fire burned in the hearth, pots hung from the walls, and the smell of herbs filled the small space. Vala sat at the table with the parchment in her hand.

"I have been waiting for you," she said. "You took longer than I expected."

"I had matters to settle." He sank down onto a wooden bench. "Have you read it?"

"There is no point until the third piece is found."

It was then that he saw the second parchment resting beneath the one in her hand.

"By the Saints! You have both pieces."

"But I don't have the other."

"Who does?"

"We will not speak of it, not now."

"Why?"

"You must know where the power is in Hafne. That is the only way. The women-"

"Women," he said and even before he said it, he knew it was not the truth but he couldn't stop himself. As much as he believed, he feared what power lay untouched on this land. "Women cook, clean, nothing more." A pain stabbed deep within his abdomen. He leaned over clutching his belly.

"Continue, my lord."

Giles struggled to regain his composure as the pain tightened deeper settling into his groin. He glanced up and met Vala's gaze.

She smiled at him. "Women are everything in Hafne."

She glanced to the parchment, seemingly dismissing him.

"Are they warriors?" he asked holding on unsteady ground.

"Are you?" She asked sweetly and laid her hand over his.

"Aye," he replied and the heat of her hand was almost his undoing. He pulled his hand free.

"No longer," she said with a look on her face that barred argument. "You are now Hafne."

The pain lifted in a dark cloud that flooded and threatened to choke him.

He reached for the parchment, the texture silky. It felt like nothing he had ever touched. Nay, that was not truth. It felt like a woman's skin. It felt like Vala.

"'Tis different than before."

"It is magical," Vala replied. "And never the same."

His index finger traced the singed edge. His face was expressionless, his eyes glassy. "He has taken the third piece far into the depths of the tower. He knows without the last piece that we are doomed."

"How?" Vala asked. "I have asked this question many times. Still, there are no answers."

"The power of the women weakened. And..." His finger pressed to the center of his forehead. "Someone showed him, a woman. I can't see her face."

"As Magna said, one of the women has turned. She would not say who."

"It does not matter. Destiny is on course. Magna has been to see Mervaine." Then reality returned and his only defense was to glare at her. God's tooth what manner of place was this when reality fought a losing battle.

"You see," Vala said softly.

"Who is he?" Giles asked. "How do I know these things for they seem fey and yet I know they are real?"

"He is the one that was banished from the land of the

Ancients."

"The Rogue," Giles added the truth coming back in uncontrolled waves of memory. "Banished by Mervaine, leader of the Ancients." He grimaced. "I remember so many things. Yet I know so little and there is no time." His head pounded with previously unknown truths.

"Mervaine has returned," Vala said with a thoughtful expression. "Magna has not said but she acts differently. I have always thought there was something more between them."

"That is between them and no consequence to what is happening here. We must prepare for Helios when the moon passes over the sun."

"Aye for it just precedes the full moon. Each of them a sign."

"You must return with me to the keep. Where you will be safe."

"No."

"You endanger your people staying here."

"No," she repeated and shook her head.

"You know I am right."

He felt her resignation for it was deep, gray and so incredibly sad that he willed himself not to shiver and shield himself and her against it.

He held out his hand. "You will keep that which roams the keep, in the keep. You will keep your people safe. Come."

"Let me gather my things."

"Before nightfall," he said as he strode from the hut.

•

"He wants me to live there."

"You knew it was only a matter of time," Magna replied.

"I can't." Vala worried her lip. "Yet I must. I fear I may not be able to resist. For he is everything and yet he is Norman."

"Every life has one great love." Magna sighed. "Mayhap ..."

Vala sank to the stool by the hearth and held her hands over the flames. She closed her eyes.

"I went to the pentagram two night's past."

"Faith, child. You entered the pentagram. It was too soon. We'll not speak of what else was there that night. You broke the spell if only for a moment."

"Giles says the circle is open."

"One circle is open but not that of the crypt. That remains

closed. What you opened lay within the first pentagram. Give the parchments to me and I shall shelter them. They will be safe for a time for the Rogue is otherwise occupied with his new possession."

It came to Vala in a flash as she stared horrified into Magna's wrinkled dear face. "The second half of the seer's stone also rested there. It was never lost. You hid it, protected by the pentagram and I opened it."

Magna sighed. "Aye. The stone is no longer there. The Rogue has grown stronger, he was able to take the stone before we realized what he was about."

"It was not you who told me go to the pentagram," Vala whispered. "By the bones, what have I done?"

"You have done only what he asked."

"The Rogue led me?"

Magna nodded. "You couldn't know. He deceives."

"I should have known. I am destined."

"You give yourself too much credit, child. He would have been as powerful as Mervaine had he been allowed to remain in Hafne. He is much more powerful than you, much older, much wiser."

Magna's rough, gnarled hand brushed gently across Vala's cheek. Magna looked to the sky. "The moon change will soon be upon us. Helios makes itself known shortly. Be ready then."

"That is no answer." Vala did not expect a reply for she did not have to look. She knew that Magna had vanished.

"I am so afraid," she whispered as around her only a trail of smoke whirled where Magna had stood.

Leave the pieces of parchment you have and I'll safeguard them. Magna's words breathed into her ear like a soft sigh or a warm caress. *You are not alone.*

•

Vala hesitated. The light from the keep's open doorway faded with every step she took. Torchlight flickered and chased shadows on the walls.

"You may set your things there." Giles appeared out of the dim recesses. In the muted light of the flickering torches, the planes of his cheeks flared strong and harsh.

"I am glad you are here. This is where you belong." He frowned. "I feel it."

"No, my Lord Giles, I belong in the village. I can't remain here overly long."

"Until I learn some truths you will stay with me. It is safer."

"Truths?"

"Who are you? Will you not tell me?"

"I already told you."

"Aye you did, Vala," his gaze caressed her. "But there is so much more," he said in a throaty caress that only made her want to kiss him, but this was not the place. Not here. Not where the other lived.

"What I know of you is only the curse of this place and naught what is here." He touched the sack that she held against her heart.

"Move aside, my lord," Vala ordered.

"Giles."

"Giles," she repeated. "Show me my pallet."

His eyebrows rose.

"Well away from yours. I shall have none of that."

His eyebrow arched higher. "None?"

"None! Not now, not here."

Come to me, my child. The sexless voice was stronger now as it wound coolly from somewhere in that distant third tower.

Vala trembled but this time the words did not draw her. She wanted to run. She wanted to return to the safety of the village but she couldn't. This was her destiny.

Chapter Twenty

"Come," he said the next morn as he took Vala's hand. "Let us break our fast."

"Nay." She shook her head. "I have already done so." She pulled her hand free. "Until you know my lord that this is not all about our desire. Until then, there can be naught between us."

"Ah, so you want me too." He reached for her and she backed up.

"Nay." She shook her head but she smiled. "As much as we both want me to say yes. I will not." And with that she pushed open the great door allowing sunshine to stream into the sullen gloom before the door banged behind her and the light went with her.

Giles joined Royce at one of the trestle tables where they broke their fast on day old bread and ale. He tore off a piece of bread before addressing Royce. "You continue work on the palisade today?"

"We are almost complete," Royce swallowed and took a pull of ale. He set the tankard down and said, "The Saxons and your squire work on the trench. It will be a first in England. I never before heard of such. A trench of water to keep marauders away, tis a good idea."

"How are you finding the villagers?" Giles asked, dispelling any farther talk of the trench. He did not want to discuss nor reveal the dream that had preceded that idea.

"They listen well enough," Royce replied. He bit into the bread, chewed and then spoke through the mouthful. "It is strange. There are few of them and unlike the women they appear to be truly Saxon."

"Uncommonly strange," Giles agreed. "But they are accepting

your command?"

"Oh aye," Royce grinned. "After I stripped the skin from the back of the last Saxon who disobeyed. I am not serious," he hastily added at the dark look Giles shot him. "I am sure had I done any such thing those women of theirs would have created a spell, cursed me, who knows.

"Do not mention curses or spells," Giles said shortly and wondered why he bothered. The place was rife with magic. He couldn't continue to accept and deny, changing his mind like the changing of the seasons. *Like a woman*, he thought as he strode from the hall.

Outside, Giles breathed in light spring air and was relieved to leave the hall's dankness. He walked over to where a group of Saxons dug the trench that would soon surround the front half of the keep.

Again Giles mulled the fact that the only males in the village were Saxon blond yet some of the women were dark and many had Norman names. He rubbed the side of his face. What went on in this village? For it seemed that many of the women were at least partly Norman and yet the men were not. Even Vala ... He paused. The facts defied all reason.

On another day, Giles would have spent time speaking to those who labored on his land, inspected the work, joined in and worked shoulder to shoulder with the laborers. Not today. Today, he wanted nothing but to ride, feel the wind on his face, eventually to find the pond that Vala had been near the other day, to find the peace and the magic of the water. He would forgo the nooning meal and ride. At the stables, Giles saddled the horse and swung himself up.

"Go on boy," he said to Ramion as they passed through the gates. Then they were in a full gallop around the village and through the open field. The wind flattened Giles' hair and the sun warmed his face. A smile pulled at his lips. He was lord of the keep. This was how he had imagined it to be. For a moment all the dark and strange moments of the last days were forgotten.

It was only after he stabled Ramion that Vala's words began to stir deep in his memories.

I did not kill the babes. What did that mean? What babes? His mind traveled over the happenings since his arrival. One babe buried. *Nay*, he thought, *two babes buried.* The first buried on the day of his arrival. On the day he saved Vala from the dunking chair. He swept the hair from his forehead. Two babes dead in such a short period. How many had there been?

He changed direction and strode toward the small copse of trees that sheltered the village's burial ground.

The trees rustled overhead and he had the distinct feeling that he was not alone. He stopped and listened but only silence surrounded him. He stepped between the shelter of the trees and into the resting place of the souls. He expected to see crosses but there were none. Instead only mounds of dirt and as he came closer, a wooden star lay flush to the soil over each resting place. There were words—indistinct markings really. He leaned closer to brush dirt and leaves from the surface of one. *Boy, born 1065 died 1065.* He moved to the next one, *Boy, born 1066, died 1066.* They were all the same, only the year sometimes changed. And in some years there were none. The sex, the fact that they were babes, all remained the same. And yet there was only one child in the village, a girl.

Giles rose. What did it all mean?

"Jesu!" his roar broke the dead's silence. "Mathilde," he rocked back on his heels. He had sent a message for her to come. "Nay," he muttered for already he knew it was too late. In a dream that was as true as his waking hours he had seen her stop at a roadside tavern. She was so close that he could feel her, close to giving birth and close to arriving here.

"God's tooth," he murmured. "What have I done?"

•

The morning light reflected gently against the surface of the pond. It was a calmness that Giles couldn't duplicate. He had sought somewhere to clear his head. He feared that he had greatly wronged his best friend's wife. He had meant to protect her after envisioning his friend's death. Instead, he had invited her here, pregnant and alone to a place where the babes all died. What else died here?

It was too late to stop Mathilde.

He swallowed heavily and tried to find peace here in the most peaceful spot he had ever known. Today there was not a ripple on the surface of the pond. The lime green leaves were brilliant under the warm early morning sun. Plants like Giles had never seen before with delicate orange flowers that rose like flutes to the sun grew around the pond. His boot chipped at the foliage and a shrill hum quavered underfoot.

He was terrified for her and her unborn babe but there was nothing he could do about Mathilde now. He had sent a messenger only an hour ago. He had hoped that the messenger reached Mathilde, that he was able to turn her away. He scuffed his foot. A leaf fluttered free and the humming intensified.

"Stop!" Vala's voice ordered from behind him. "They are magic, healing, and very much alive. They cry to you."

"The plants cry! God's teeth woman!" Giles swung around. "Where did you come from?"

"No matter. The place is magical and must be respected."

"Leave me," he grated. He couldn't take much more for she was like a siren's call, all temptation and he wanted so much more than to take her into his arms. He wanted everything. Instead, he strode toward the woods.

But she followed and memories of that first day, when he had thought her to be naught but a fey fairy, made him reach for her despite his best intentions.

"We wage the same war, you, I, the village." He tried cajoling her into his arms.

"War?" Her brows arched and she danced out of reach. "T'will not happen. Not now."

Thunder cracked overhead. Lightning flashed and purple tinged the yellow spikes of jagged light.

He sighed. The woman was impossible. "Tell me about the Ancients and this land."

"The Ancients have always been here." Vala cleared her throat. "But you already know about the Ancients.

"Some. Tell me the rest."

"They lived here before anyone, before recorded time. They are not human and can't die. But now it is different. They are no longer physical beings, except for Magna." Vala paused. "I don't know what I would do without her, she is always there for me."

"And damned annoying."

"Magna guides us to our destiny. The others too, but only in spirit."

"Wulfgar was the last to hold this keep. He has something to do with the prophecy, with the curse?" Giles asked.

"Wulfgar was Saxon but it was his betrayal of Hafne, he gave the keep and all it holds to the Normans, that was the final of the three prophesized betrayals and began the curse. I discovered he was meeting with Normans. At night he would slip out. I—"

"You knew that he would betray you all," Giles added, thoughts of desire gone.

"I would not allow the steward to keep any further records. I knew Wulfgar would use what he had to betray us. If we looked as if we didn't prosper, than maybe... But still there was him and he didn't care about records."

"Him?"

"The Rogue of the Ancients. The one who we all fear." She paused. "I have known of him all my life. Legend has it that the Rogue was the first Norman-Saxon Ancient to bear full power of the Ancients. He was the result of a Norman taking a woman of Hafne against her will. When he was ten, he killed his mother. The Ancients acknowledged then what he would become and had him banished. Mervaine took his name and with that eternal life. He in turn cursed this land." She paused. "He has found a way to live through the generations and now he is here."

Giles waited as Vala glanced around the clearing before her attention again returned to him. "Tell me how Wulfgar betrayed Hafne." He cleared his throat, the name of this place raw and rough on his tongue.

"A boat was beached on the shore and," she stared into the distance, "Wulfgar went down to meet them. They were all armed, warriors ... and Norman."

"And you saw no need to alert anyone? Tell me your reason," he commanded.

"I didn't want to jeopardize my mother."

"Your mother?" He tried to contain his shock. "She was there." It was a fact. He knew it as he stated it.

"Wulfgar followed one of the Normans back to the crypt. It was so cold."

She clutched her upper arms as if she relived what she had once seen.

"The Norman seemed to disappear." She frowned. "It was almost like he became the shadow that covered Wulfgar. What happened next, I have never forgotten. Wulfgar stepped into the pentagram. It got so cold it felt one could die of it and then there was nothing. When I awoke it was silent and Wulfgar and my mother dead."

"When was that?"

"Twelve turns of the moon before the invasion."

"The year of Our Lord 1065," he said thoughtfully.

"By the time I got out of the crypt the boats were gone. It was as if it had never happened. I spent the night searching. There was nothing until dawn. Then Magna arrived and we found his body," Vala said. She added. "Before it again disappeared."

"His body?"

"He was dead. His skin was white, so white." The last trailed in a whisper. "Magna found his skin branded with a mark. I've never seen her react like that. Her face aged and faded so fast I thought that I had lost her and then she only said one thing."

She paused over the next words for they came painfully to her. "He returns."

Vala twisted the ring.

"If I were you, I would remove that." He pointed to the ring. "It is drawing evil to you as you wear it. They know you by the ring." He dashed a hand across his eyes as pain swept across his forehead.

"He is supposed to be drawn to this. For without him knowing me, I can't destroy him."

"Destroy him? You! Saints, you are only a woman and from what I have learned that which haunts this land has much power."

"Will have much power but not yet." She raised a hand and he humored her with silence for the moment. "Magna and the others guide me."

"Come." The command was etched with fire that he hoped hid his uneasiness. He lifted her and set her on Ramion's back before jumping on ahead of her.

"Hang on," he said as the horse began to gallop.

Her hands tugged at his tunic and then her arms wrapped around him. Soft curves pressed into his back and he desperately tried to think of other things as his body followed its own path of attraction.

Ahead the keep loomed and faintly behind the second tower, a third.

"Jesu," he muttered.

And it was with relief that they finally reached the keep for there was only so much a man could take. As he slid off Ramion and reached for her, the third tower winked in the sunlight and vanished. Now there were only two. There were always only two. His need for Vala was blurring his reality. None of this was true. And to prove it he took her in his arms and kissed her.

•

The Rogue moved throughout the keep keeping far away from those that now lived and shared his space. He hated it, hated them. but it would not be for much longer. His time was close. The sun would soon darken the land and then there was only the full moon to await and then she would choose him. He opened his palm and the stone blinked brightly at him. Above him the singed timbers reminded him of that day when he had received enough life energy to return. When the fires had flickered and the wood had burned in brilliant flares of light.

Flesh of his flesh.

His strength was the girl. She offered eternal life. Together they would be more powerful than ever an Ancient had been.

He slid back through the hidden passage where he spent his days and much of his nights as his strength grew. The stench of decay swept around him. He closed his eyes and sucked in a deep breath. It was the closest thing to ambrosia he had smelled in years.

Chapter Twenty-one

"Editha," Vala began. "We must speak."

Editha stopped chopping and laid the knife aside.

"You want to ask about him, he that was my husband." Editha stated. She looked up at Giles. "You have finally seen the truth."

"At least some of it," Giles agreed.

Editha nodded. "Here. Let us sit by the fire. The warmth always makes things easier to speak of difficult things. Come." Editha led the way to the three-legged stools that flanked the fire pit. "Sit," she directed gruffly.

"Your husband, he was Norman. Was he not?" Giles asked. The question had been burning deep within him for many days.

"Ahhh, Ranulf. He was beautiful to look at. One wouldn't think so, not of one married to such as me," Editha smiled sheepishly. "Aye." A dreamy look came over her face. "He was. Until the time he disappeared he was a good husband. I had no complaints."

"We have never spoken of the men that left," Vala replied and glanced at Giles before turning her attention back to Editha. "I am sorry for making you speak of such now. Of causing you hurt but I have only known because of Magna and because ..."

"Of your sight," Editha replied. "I'll speak of him and of the Others. There are some things that mayhap even you do not know."

"Men of Norman blood," Vala stared into the dancing flames.

"Aye," Editha replied. "Both Cecile and I believe there was a pact before their birth."

"Destined," Vala breathed and glanced at Giles. He was watching Editha intently.

"Nay," Editha shook her head. "Chosen, like you, but they chose wrong." She closed her eyes and held her hands before the fire.

"How many are there?" Vala asked.

"Their numbers have dwindled. But recently there are more, Alfred, the false priest, and of course the creature." Editha's mouth turned down in distaste. "The thing has the blood of him, the Rogue."

"The men were gone before I arrived," Vala said. "Yet still there are so few."

"For a time only girls were born," Editha said sadly.

"There are many babes buried here," Giles said, his voice oddly thick.

"Aye, boys to begin, then girls. That is why there are many young women in this village and few men of any age."

"Yet, I never asked," Vala said softly.

"It was not the time."

"When did Ranulf leave?"

"They left the spring of 1064," Editha replied. "I'll never forget that day," she murmured. "Ranulf had begun acting uncommonly strange months before. As had Albert, Cecile's husband. Neither of us thought much of it. We had other things to think of. Both of us awaited babes in the fall." Editha glanced to the mud dabbled ceiling. "And, of course our other children were still young."

"Ranulf left in the night. There was no goodbye. Together a dozen left. Of course some have died since. Theirs was not an easy choice." She pushed a stick into the fire. "They left in the morning," Editha swallowed. "This is what is so strange. We knew. Before even Cecile had spread the runes, we knew."

"Cecile?" Vala asked. "She must have been a different woman from who I've come to know."

"Very," Editha replied. "She was much like me. We were good friends. Until the men left."

"And then?"

"Then, the howls began deep in the woods at night. The crop failed that year. The seed had come up, the rains occurred but the plants all died. Then you arrived only days after the men left. Just as it was prophesized, just as Magna always said."

"Then Wulfgar died and he arrived."

"In 1065, one year after you arrived. The Rogue was what our men waited for." Editha swallowed. "It was hard for I loved Ranulf once. After the babe died, even though Ranulf was already gone, everything changed."

"A babe?"

"It was a male babe," Editha said without emotion. "The first such to die in Hafne."

"You birthed a babe. A male," Vala whispered. "The first of Ancient, Norman, Saxon blood. The first since the final betrayal." She rose from the stool and knelt in front of Editha. "Oh Editha, I am so sorry. I was too young to realize. Too caught in my own grief. To think your babe was the first, the one who began it all."

"You were a child yourself mourning the death of a mother. There was naught you could do."

"Are you saying that this village is not completely human? That tis just not Saxons and Normans but something unearthly?" Giles voice rose a notch and he stood up. "Tis unbelievable."

"As unbelievable as Magna and you have seen her," Vala replied calmly.

Giles sat back down.

Vala clasped Editha's hands. "There is more."

"Cecile also birthed a babe, that same week."

"I remember," Vala said softly. "Sibley."

"Aye," Editha replied softly. "Sibley. The last babe with the blood of the three, the last babe of Hafne."

"By the gods!" Vala dropped Editha's hands and stood. "She too is chosen!"

"No," Editha shook her head. "She is not. But she is special in her own way. That is all I know of the child."

"The Others?"

"My love died for Ranulf that spring when I watched Wulfgar die. It was only then that I realized why our last child died. For that night I heard their cries of celebration deep in the forest. He caused my child to die. He and the group of men he left me for." She rose and turned her back to the fire, chafing her hands together. "So that is the way of it. For these many years they have lived in the forest answering the commands of he who lives in the tower. They were chosen and they accepted his call."

"Ahh, Editha," Vala said. She folded her hands. "Yet I am a birther and all I have birthed are babes that do not live."

"There is a reason that it is you."

"I do not know how you have born it so long, Editha."

"I do not need your sympathy, only your courage." Editha glared at her. "You are our birther because one day there will be babes in Hafne."

"Some days I lose hope," Vala murmured.

Editha took her hands in both of hers. "You will save Hafne, Vala, you and …" She looked at Giles and smiled. "You and Lord Giles. You must find the way." She sat back, releasing Vala. "Now, go, I am overtired and I still have the meal to prepare."

Editha went back to the vegetables she was chopping.

Vala watched her thoughtfully even as Giles pulled her to her feet. And even with him by her side, her steps were heavy, weighed down by a destiny to large to comprehend.

◆

"These men must die. Yet they were once dear to the women." Giles said later as they walked back to the keep. He stopped and looked down at Vala. "What say you?"

"That does not matter."

"Nay, it matters greatly. I can't kill these men unless …" He rubbed the side of his jaw leaving the sentence unfinished.

"Unless what?"

"They agree."

"Who?"

"The women. As long as it matters not to them whether these men live or die, they will die," Giles said.

"I'll talk to the women. We'll prepare for battle." Vala dusted her hands down the side of her tunic.

"Prepare? Have you lost all reason? Women do not battle."

"Do not battle elsewhere, my lord. But in Hafne things are very different."

She smiled slowly up at him and his hands ached to gather her close and feel her sweetness pressed tight against him.

"I do not mean battle such as you think. Ours is a battle without mace or sword." She moved away and her bare feet seemed to glide over the grass.

"I do not understand."

"I will not follow you to battle with the Others. That, for now, is all you need."

His attention returned to Vala. Her eyes gleamed with the talk of battles ahead while her hair blew free with the wimple long forgotten days ago. Somehow sharing power did not seem such a foreign thought, not totally. Not today.

He shook his head in a desperate attempt to right his wayward thinking. Men ruled, they always had and they always would. But these women challenged everything he believed.

Giles followed Vala's gaze. She seemed to be staring at a point just beyond the second tower.

"The stone makes the difference. It gives him the power he needs. He is no longer dependent." Vala remained fixed on the towers.

"Jesu, he has one of the stones?"

"The night in the pentegram. He led me there but was only strong enough to steal the stone, not the piece of parchment."

"I shall steal it from him."

"You can't, not yet."

"What then? Do nothing? That is ridiculous."

"The stones are attracted to each other. Where is yours? Do you still carry it?"

"That is safest. When even a pentagram was violated."

"I opened it," Vala said softly.

"You were tricked. He was powerful even before."

"Still."

"We must tread softly on the arrival of Helios." His face was again cast in that faraway look. "His power will increase."

She glanced to Giles and his eyes met hers.

"There is more to the prophecy and our destiny than you think," he whispered.

"And less than you would like," Vala shot back.

The Ancients' cackles filled the empty sky.

•

Giles strode to the village where the women gathered as usual near the well. Lately they were always in a group. In a flash decision he gave up the idea of individual interviews.

"It has taken you longer than we anticipated," said a small woman. She faced him, her head uncovered and her hair hanging in a single braid down her back.

"You have expected me." Giles was not surprised.

"Of course," Editha said from the other side of the well. "The runes were spilled many days ago. This too was prophesied."

"So then you will know how this mystery ends."

"If only, my lord," the women spoke as one.

"Your men that have left you, tell me about them."

"The older among us, our men have been dead to us for many years," Editha said.

"Aye," another woman said sadly. "They were weak."

"Destined," said another.

"Now what once we loved longs only to see our end."

"I hate him," another said.

"I do not hate," Editha said. "When I feel anything it is only sadness and fear. He is dead to me but if would be so much better if that were true."

"I'll end it," Giles said. "I needed to know how you felt."

"You cared for our feelings?"

"Of course. You are my people."

"Do not ride into the wood alone. We will—" Editha began.

"Nay! I do not need women to wage a battle." He shook his head unable to believe the audacity.

"Ahh, my lord. You need us much more than you are aware. But soon you will learn the truth of the women of Hafne. We are warriors." And Editha walked away.

"Warriors." Giles shrugged his shoulders, shaking off the foolish talk. It was time to get ready for battle.

But at noon all work stopped and the villagers clustered anxiously in the bailey.

"What is wrong?" Royce turned to Giles.

"The sun, Helios." Vala came up beside them. "Our destiny is near."

The moon was clear in the sky as it slid slowly toward the sun. The land began to darken and the voices became more anxious. A few minutes later the sun disappeared and the land became as dark as pitch.

"The gods have deserted us," one elderly man cried. "What have we done?"

"Do not look at the sky!" Giles roared. He had a clear image of what would happen when the sun returned. He had seen this happen once before.

The frightened talk continued as if he had never spoken.

Vala raised her hand. Giles was sure he could hear a hum. When he looked toward her he felt peace emanate from her.

"The sun will return," she said so softly that except for the dense quiet, one would have had to strain to hear. She reached for Giles' hand. And as her soft skin folded against his, energy swept through him, hot, sweet and powerful. The time had arrived. "Do not look at it for the brilliance will blind you."

As the sun began to shine again Giles saw a pinwheel of light that did not seem to originate from the sun. He swung around and dropped Vala's hand. The light flared across the keep. Three wheels of light shafted across the crumbling stone of the two towers.

"The sign. It is the sign!" someone shouted.

Giles froze. Behind the two towers of the keep was a third, clear and outlined by the sun as it blazed overhead.

"Jesu," he breathed.

On the rampart his men bunched in a group and it was immediately apparent that Gilroy was missing.

"He looked into the eye of the sun. The young fool," Giles muttered.

The mysterious tower will wait, he thought as he rushed up the ladder to the palisade. Gilroy was sprawled on the wooden run, his knuckles pressed against his eyes.

"I can't see," he repeated again and again.

Gently, Giles pulled the man's fists from his eyes. "Can you open your eyes at all?"

"Spots," Gilroy moaned. "I see spots. I am blind."

Giles smiled, relieved that the man was not totally blinded. "I told you not to look, yet you did. Royce get him to the keep," Giles commanded.

"You will see again," he said to Gilroy. He glanced to Magna. "Your sight in the next turn of the moon." He drew back. Where had that come from? He strode toward the keep but Magna's words trailed after him.

I couldn't have prophesized better, Magna chuckled. *My work is almost done.* The laughter had not left her voice before she disappeared.

Beside him Royce stared curiously at a spot near Giles where Magna had stood. "My eyesight must be failing," he muttered.

Giles said, "You saw the hag?"

Royce frowned. "I saw nothing. Only my imagination." He looked askance to Giles.

"She was real."

"I need ale," Royce replied.

"You will need many cups of ale if you are going to herald Magna's appearance with ale."

"No human appears at will," Royce's voice was thick, shaky.

"She is no human," Giles replied. "Some day I'll explain all to you." He left Royce and went over to the keep where the women were gathered.

•

"The time is short. You must find Vala quickly," Editha said.

"Vala?" he asked as he only now realized that she had disappeared.

"There. You must go." Editha pointed to the clear sky behind the towers. "To the third tower."

Magna appeared from nowhere. "Find Vala. Know what she knows, what she learns. You must hurry. Go."

Who was in charge here? His thoughts pummeled him as his feet followed the women's orders. The women had commanded and he had obeyed.

I, Giles de Montford, would rule Hafne, he thought as he strode in the direction the women had ordered.

Always, have the women had power. Magna's voice whispered to him. *Is that such a bad thing?*

No, Giles acknowledged. *For now, it's not.*

He smiled as he saw Vala on the threshold of the keep. As always, she was barefoot. Her hands drifted through her rumpled hair as she muttered. Her words were vague, hazy. She appeared like one in a trance. Finally, she lifted her head. Her eyes were clouded as if in the aftermath of a dream.

"This is the first chance we have had to enter the third tower," she said. "There are many answers there. It is up to you and me. I know not how. I wish it were not so. I dreamt— Never mind, such as you would not understand."

"Maybe I would. I dream too. Dreams that come true."

"Come," Vala commanded sharply, the dream cloud gone from her eyes.

Chapter Twenty-two

Giles followed her outside the keep and through a small passageway that led back inside the keep. He hadn't known this existed. He had been here many times and there had only been rock and the vine that grew in the shade of this wall, nothing else. Within the passage light danced from the walls and glared brilliantly at the other end. Overhead, he looked up and could see the sky. It was as if the keep did not exist.

"This is not possible," he muttered.

She clasped his hand and said, "It is possible. The world of the Ancients overlaps ours. This is just your first glimpse of it." She squeezed his hand. "He, the Rogue," she amended. "Was also Ancient. His reality is mixed with ours."

Giles said nothing for he couldn't. The energy that flooded through him at her touch was stronger than before. It was like he had become part of her and the feeling was as heady as it was incomprehensible.

She stopped as they had reached the end of the passage. They both looked upward where an ancient ladder propped against nothing and tilted into the sky. Overhead a faint outline shadowed the ladder, a cloud or maybe a floor, it was hard to tell as everything blurred into one. He shook his head but his vision wouldn't clear.

"Do you see?" Vala whispered for the floor was now sheeted in gold that sparkled in the sunlight.

A chuckle wove around them, the gold disappeared and the floor became transparent. A fire blazed in a hearth and a robed figure stood before the fire warming its hands. Slowly it turned but the face was still hidden by a cowl. It beckoned to them with a seductive quirk of its finger.

Giles glanced upward. There was nothing but a room of wood so old that light shone through the breaks and cracks. The cowled figure, the fire, they were all gone.

Vala began to climb the ladder.

He reached for her. She should not go first into the unknown, into danger. His hands clasped her waist. His foot slipped on the bottom rung.

"I'm sorry Vala," he called faintly as they fell. The fall took forever yet they had only climbed a few rungs of the ladder. Air rushed and passed them and the sweet scent of honey filled his senses. Then the sensations ended and air whooshed from his lungs as he landed on hard stone. Vala landed with a delicious thump in the middle of his chest and strangely her weight hitting him was more provocative than uncomfortable.

Vala turned over. "Are you hurt?"

Giles grunted.

Vala's face hovered only inches over his.

Finally he was able to draw in air. He had no sooner sucked in that first delicious breath before her lips skimmed his. They were gentle, yet evocative. His hands lifted to pull her to him but his arms were too slow to meet his commands.

Breasts pressed against him and then were gone as Vala rolled off of him.

"You lumbering ox. You are not quick enough to go first." She turned around and made for the ladder.

"Vala, no!" Giles struggled to his feet.

"Catch me," she teased as milky light bathed her features.

This felt like nowhere else and Vala's reaction was strangely un-Vala-like. Giles didn't care. He wouldn't pass up an invitation to seduction. Not with Vala. Not with the woman who he would one day wife.

"You will marry me."

Why had he said that? Birds chirped overhead and the sweet scent of honey was again everywhere.

"Nay, Norman," she called cheerfully. "But thank you for the offer."

Above, where there had once been nothing, he could see the floor of the tower. It was old, dusty and empty.

"I was serious."

"I know. But this is not reality. Think of Magna. The magic is not so apt to control you then," she called over her shoulder.

He tried to think of the hag. He really did as he grasped the ladder and began to climb. But Vala's pert backside wiggled seductively against the tight boy's tunic and prevented any thought at all.

The woman was an enticing little piece. He picked up his pace, as he was anxious to catch her, to make her pay in the sweetest way possible for causing him such agony.

Giles stepped into an empty room of dull, old wood. In the darkness something scratched as if being dragged across the wood and then there was nothing except the steady, distant, yet familiar sound of the sea.

It was a large room, much like the two other towers. There was a broken hearth at one end and nothing else.

"God's tooth that climb was so short and yet never ended! What goes here?"

The scent of honey and warmth, deep and comforting, flooded the room.

Giles prowled the tower. Vala followed. The roof was partially missing as were part of the walls. Yet the bailey couldn't be seen. Instead, emerald green groves of trees, sparkling blue water above which large birds with red beaks screeched from the trees and a peaceful hum of voices wafted around them. It was like what he had seen at the pond had taken over the entire land.

"Hafne, as it was," Vala said as she came up beside him.

"The keep sits on Hafne land, the land of the Ancients," Giles replied. "It has taken me many days to admit this."

"And yet you must."

"Among so many other things." Giles reached for her. Meaning to pull her to him, keep her safe, to love her.

God's tooth! His thoughts interjected into his increasingly foggy reality. *Get control of yourself man. Women will control you if you let them. Never that.* He backed away from her.

Fool! A malice stained voice chuckled.

They must leave. The thought was sudden and followed immediately by the delicate scent of honey. His blood seemed to heat, thicken and his limbs slowed. He swallowed heavily, desperately.

He looked to Vala. They must leave and he couldn't move.

"Vala," was all Giles could say, and in that one word was all the need and want that churned within him. "Vala," he choked. He who led was now being well and sweetly led. The scent of honey was thick, syrupy, intoxicating. "Vala," the word was drawn out.

She looked to him but her face held no emotion. She held out her hand and her lips moved. He reached and their fingers touched.

"Vala," he said thickly, "I need you."

The room seemed to shrink around them. A shiver traveled Giles' spine and he shuddered.

"I don't know what to do." It was the hardest thing he had ever said and yet here in the unreal intimacy of the third tower it was possible.

Their fingers seductively grazed, skin on skin.

Waves lapped on a distant shore and beneath his feet the mellow wood trembled.

"Vala," he was reduced to only repeating her name.

"I want you," she said thickly. And magic settled into the bones of the third tower.

The scent of honey was almost overpowering and interlaced within that scent was a hint of lavender.

There was no dance of seduction. No dance was needed. The magic had done that these last moments as their senses were seduced, assaulted and seduced again.

Her tunic whispered as the cloth swished around her body and her limbs carried her closer to him.

"Norman," she said softly.

Mayhap he was the one, the one to take her here. But his hands did not touch the ties of her tunic. Instead her hands cupped his face and her body slid seductively against his.

"No," she murmured against his lips.

Like the land starved for rain or a bee at a flower he sucked the sweet honey from her lips. Her tongue dueled with his and then she nipped his lower lip as her tongue seductively stroked.

"Norman, for now you are mine."

The inflection was unfamiliar, unlike Vala. Yet he couldn't break away. Everything about this place was different. He was different. His body trembled as her hands slid down his throat. As her hands undid the lace thong of his tunic and bared his chest.

His tunic dropped to the ground.

Her fingers drifted light kisses along his chest. The sweet agony was too exquisite to break. He let her lead. This seduction was hers and it was bliss.

Her soft lips trembled light kisses down his overheated flesh. His new role of passive follower was too erotic to end.

She unlaced her tunic. The material pooled, slowly from her body revealing her creamy shoulders, the puckered need of her sweet breasts seductively veiled by her golden hair. He had to drag his eyes from her. He swallowed, regained control and met her gaze. She was completely, gorgeously naked.

He did nothing. He couldn't. He was caught in the mire of languid desire and something else.

Her smile was seductive and so unlike Vala. It didn't matter for he was fully and completely mesmerized.

The scent of honey and warmth disappeared and suddenly he stood in a broken tower with a naked woman and reality—Vala.

In a place that should not exist the beauty of her naked form seemed like nothing created on earth. He swallowed heavily and it seemed that all his saliva had dried up. His throat was parched.

Her arms lifted around his neck and only the barrier of his hose remained. Again her breasts pressed softly, provocatively against the tautness of his skin. Again, she pulled away.

"Nay, Vala I can't stand this. Please." The words tore from him.

Silently she molded his hose with her slender fingers, cupped him briefly and pulled the hose down. Again her body was fast against his as they slid to the floor.

"Now, my lord," she whispered as her tongue skirted his ear.

Her thighs clasped tight around him. It was exquisite. It was mindless. It was torture. It was over before it had hardly begun.

"Jesu," he moaned through clenched teeth. "I am sorry, Vala." She was his undoing. He was like an untried boy. Passion began to fade.

"Again," she whispered and took him into her hand. That was all he needed. The scent of honey was everywhere. Her lips trailed down his chest and her tongue flitted seductively against his nipple. She nipped with her teeth and soothed with her tongue. His hand reached for her breast. She nipped harder.

"Nay, my lord. Remember," she chuckled softly.

It was too much. His entire body throbbed. He groaned.

And he did not think it was possible but then none of this was real, and he couldn't imagine how it could be any better. But it was so much better. For this time she rode him.

She exhausted him, drained him, never had he felt so sated. He had not thought he could be called to battle that frequently in such a short period. Never before in all his life, it was wondrous. She was wondrous. He stroked her cheek and his hand trailed hesitantly along her creamy shoulder. She gazed down on him. Her thighs gently bracketing his chest, her sweet derriere warmly pressed against him.

"You my lord," she whispered the same words that had directed their seduction from the beginning. "Are mine."

Before he could summon the strength to pull his hose on, she was dressed and gone. Giles remained where she had left him, stunned. Like the dreams when she had made love to him, the reality had been exactly the same.

•

On the last rung of the ladder Vala stopped. Her hands trembled as reality began to return. Still birds chirped songs the like of which she had never heard before. A tremulous hum began swirl around her.

No.

It was a soft call, distant. A denial that did not hold rage but Vala knew it soon would.

She couldn't leave him. For the voice that called was no friend of Giles.

"Giles," she called softly reluctant to return, reluctant to face what it all might mean.

"Giles," she called again before reluctantly beginning to climb the ladder. She found him staring over the broken wall with a perplexed expression on his face.

He glanced down at her as she came to his side. "Hafne, it is still there," he murmured and placed an arm around her shoulders.

"We must leave. What was done should not have happened here." She grasped his hand. "Come, we must leave."

Overhead a Grechner flew, low, shadowing their faces. It hovered above for a long moment while time seemed to hang still. Then, with a screech it flew off.

"Jesu!" Giles muttered. "What was that?"

"A Grechner, sacred to Hafne."

"The magic?"

"Is here," Vala finished.

But for now even the magic faded as the wood rotted and disintegrated beneath their feet. By the time they reached the bottom rung of the ladder, the tower was gone. As if it had all been a dream, a ripe and luscious dream.

"Real or a dream?" Vala whispered.

"Both," Giles replied and took her hand.

•

She had mated with the Norman.

The Rogue gritted his teeth at the thought. Even though there was no harm in it, even though he had encouraged their lust, speeded the passage with the aphrodisiacs gained through the ages. Somehow she thought that passion was the antidote for the curse, part of the prophecy. She was wrong.

Yet it was good that she used her lust. It confused the Norman. That was the only reason he had left them alone to use his space, that and his lingering weakness. His energy must be conserved.

Nay, there was nothing wrong with a little lust. Humans had gotten one thing right. He chuckled as he glided around the perimeter of his tower, lifting the humors that their joining had left and sending them flying back to the space inhabited by humans. When he was done, his tower was again pristine, filled only with the scent of rot and decay that had become his aphrodisiac.

Chapter Twenty-three

"We ride tomorrow," Giles said the next day as he settled across from Royce at the trestle table.

"For?" Royce glanced up from the mug of ale he had been seriously inspecting.

"The woods."

"The Others."

"How do you know of them?"

"The walls weep with secrets," Royce said.

Giles rose. "We ride before the sun sets tomorrow."

"The woods at dark?"

"To roust the Others we must find them as they gather at dark," Giles said, using the knowledge he had gleaned from talking to the women.

Royce's face lost color.

"They are only a group of misfits that terrorize the village. Nothing we can't overcome."

"Nay," Royce shook his head. "Tis more than that."

"Mayhap you are right," Giles replied thoughtfully. "Only recently I saw fear on Vala's face."

"Vala, ah, so that is the way of it."

"Do not speak foolishness," Giles retorted. "The woman is an enticing piece," he replied with forced nonchalance.

"So you say but you also need a wife," Royce replied.

"There is no time to consider such things. Not now. Soon we'll raid the camp of those that terrorize my people."

Royce lifted his mug. "I never regretted a moment."

"What foolishness do you speak?"

"I do not have a good feeling about this, Giles."

"It is nothing but a small skirmish. You worry like an old woman."

"Perhaps you are right."

"I am," Giles said firmly. "You are uneasy before every battle. This is not even a battle."

"No matter what happens, I would not have had it any other way."

"God's tooth man, there are few that we ride against. You have fought bigger battles single handed." He clapped a hand on Royce's shoulder. "Have another cup of ale, steady your nerves," he joked. "Thank God the Saxons know how to keep a good store of ale." He raised his tankard. "To a rousing battle. And to success."

"Success," Royce echoed.

That night, Giles slid the ring on his finger. A ring like the half of the seer's stone generations of women had carried through the ages. Again, he was the first male. A fact he did not fully understand nor question. He couldn't have verbalized his motivation but his heart told him it was right.

•

The next day, in the early evening Giles inspected his gathered men. They would ride on the Others this night.

"Open the gates," Giles shouted.

The iron wheel began to churn, metal grating. The huge wood gates slowly opened like gigantic petals on a flower.

Without looking he knew that she was beside him. The scent of meadow and lavender followed her. "Be careful," she said softly.

"And you." He leaned close. "Remain far away from the crypt, the tower, and the pentagram. Wait for me."

"There is nothing I can do now without you. Willa spilled the runes this morning."

Warm breath fanned his ear. *Watch your back for the one called Ewaldo, the creature.* And again there was nothing, Magna was nowhere in sight.

"Hurry back," Vala said reluctantly. "There is much work for us to do."

"A night or two at most," he promised.

"Be careful," she whispered. "He would have you dead."

"Have no fear."

"But I do. He is getting so much stronger. I can feel his

strength."

"As can I," Giles replied. "You too must be careful, very careful." He leaned closer to her and his lips brushed against her ear and again, as was so common in this place, his will seemed to belong to someone else. "I am still in need of a wife."

Vala jerked away.

And he frowned. What had he said? "Be careful," he repeated. "Keep my bed warm." And he saluted her as he rode out.

•

"I am still in need of a wife." The words played over and over again in her mind.

Vala watched Giles mount, raise his hand and move forward with his men without a backward glance and her heart clenched. She prayed to the gods that he returned safely and she feared that wasn't enough. Tears rose unbidden and choking as she swallowed them back. She couldn't lose him. She wiped her eyes with the back of her hand and took a deep breath. For not only was he chosen, she needed him.

The keep rose dark and foreboding, and empty. Vala stared up into the parapets as a shadow drifted across.

Come to me. The thready voice called.

Nay, Vala shook her head.

Behind her Magna cackled.

Vala swung around to face the old woman. "Why do you laugh?"

"I laugh because yet again you try to deceive yourself." She pointed a knobby finger up to where Vala had seen the shadow. "He is as real as the two of us."

•

While in the woods that night Giles dreamt of Vala as around him everything was unnaturally quiet. It was as if when night fell everything ran for cover, for the safety of their respective lairs. Giles and his men found nothing that night.

He was still in need of a wife, that was what he had told Vala and it was true. He would marry her. He loved her. He considered for a moment. He hadn't told her such and mayhap he should. For once, the thought of a battle didn't thrill him. He only wanted to get back to her. To show her the love he felt and to make love to her. For that was the only way he knew how to tell her what was in his heart.

The next day they found the clearing. In the center the grass was trampled. Black cloth fluttered on a low hanging branch. The remains of a stale fire's ashes sprawled within a circle of stones.

"They will return here tonight." The stone hummed within its pouch. Giles stroked the stone, taking comfort in its warmth. "We'll rest. Tonight we battle."

His hand trembled as the stone sang of truth and something else, a prickle of foreboding.

Later in the evening, against the backdrop of the moon in the starless sky, smoke plumes rose and nosed the forest canopy.

"I see nothing, Giles. I am lost within this dark maze."

"Nay, Royce, see the smoke. They are ahead," Giles whispered.

Time seemed immutable as they crawled through the foliage. The seer's stone thrummed in its pouch and Giles dared not touch it for it was too hot. Instead the pouch burned against his thigh.

Giles stopped and his men piled in behind him. Through the brush and campfire smoke, foggy figures hummed an unknown chant. The smoke thinned. A group of cowled men sat around a crackling fire. They continued to hum their unearthly tune even though they must know that armed men flanked them. The cowled hoods over their heads hid their identity and their sex, yet Giles knew they were all male. These were the Others. Giles was sure of it. The cowled figures raised their hands, each one linked to the man beside him and turned as one.

"Who is your leader?" Giles demanded.

They raised their linked hands higher. The fire crackled and roared and a log sank into the fire and sent sparks high into the night sky.

"Your campaign of fear is at an end. The spells you cast to kill the babes, over," Giles predicted.

"Think you," said one who dropped the hand of the men on either side and rose to confront Giles, "de Montford, a mere Norman. Do you think you can stop one such as he? He is all. He is everything."

"Good will prevail!" the men proclaimed.

"Good!" The man who had first spoken threw the cowl back from his head and spat, "The only thing that will prevail is the one now only called Rogue, soon his name will be known to all. Soon, you will be dead. To arms!" he bellowed.

The roar was that of a warrior, and that startled Giles. But before he could consider that, the group was on its feet as one and rushing forward. Swords were pulled from their robes, spells forgotten.

Dark haired every one, here were the men, the Norman mix of Hafne. Hafne that ancient land of magic. The thoughts were fleeting and quickly ended as he bellowed his cry to arms and charged.

But the Others rushed en masse away from Giles. Before Giles realized what they were about they had surrounded Royce. It was sudden, unexpected and all he could do was lead his men into the crush.

Giles fought furiously, clearing a swathe as men dropped. The battle was intense but brief. There were too few opponents. It was an easy battle. One he couldn't wait to jest with Royce about on their return to the keep. A cowled figure screamed as he went down and overhead a tremendous screeching filled the air. When it was over the Others lay dead.

Giles sheathed his sword. "We'll return to the keep come first light." He looked around. "No one was hurt?" he asked.

"No," Turstin said. "We are all unscathed. It was an easy but strange battle."

Robert strode toward him. "The bodies?"

"Burn them and bury the remains," Giles said as he glanced toward the fire. "They no longer belong to Hafne. They are dead to all."

"Hafne?" Robert asked puzzled.

"The name of this land," Giles said and turned away meaning to take a closer look at what had been the hideaway of the group.

"de Montford." His name sounded like bereavement as it trembled in the clearing.

As if in slow motion, he turned. And the truth hit him in a brief flash of intuition and the stone's piercing heat.

"Nay!" Giles roared. He charged forward where the men were beginning to gather around one body. Giles pushed forward to where Royce lay.

"I am sorry, Giles," Royce muttered as Giles gently lifted Royce's head from the ground, from the pool of blood that gathered around him.

And even as he looked at him, Giles knew it was too late. Even his ability to heal could do nothing now.

"You fought a good battle," Giles replied thickly with his friend's head resting in his lap. The rest of the men gathered, some kicked the cowled bodies away. They watched as Royce breathed his last and as Giles gently lifted him from amidst the evil in which he had fought.

Chapter Twenty-four

They had ridden hard the last few hours. Their mounts were lathered and winded, and the men parched. They galloped the short distance to the keep. Giles leapt from Ramion's back even as they reached the outer walls. Beyond them the keep rose gray and bleak, and as if nothing had changed. Yet everything had. Behind the second tower he saw a faint glow, the third tower. He broke into a run. One name replayed itself over and over through his mind, *Vala*.

As the keep door began to creak open he was already pushing it open. He couldn't wait to see her, to hold her. He strode in and immediately swept her into his arms.

"Are you hurt?" His lips claimed hers before she could answer. His arms tried to pull her tighter, to show her the love that welled from him.

But she pulled away and glanced up the stairs. "Giles, the other women are at the village. I am alone."

"What are you saying?" He frowned and would have thought it an invitation except for the tears that shimmered in her eyes. "Vala, what's wrong?"

"Anne," she said softly. "She's dead."

"Anne." It took a moment for that truth to sink in and for another reality to shift amidst the grief and love and relief that churned in an emotional cauldron within his breast. His love for Vala, his worry for her, his grief for Royce and now this, for a moment he could scarcely breathe. And when he did his instincts only screamed to hold her. This time when he took her in his arms she did not resist. Within in the circle of his arms he could feel her shoulders shake as she softly cried.

"Vala." He held her tight and whispered against her ear.

With her usual fortitude she pushed back from him but still he held her loosely in the circle of his arms.

"I found her here."

"Dead?"

"Nay." She shook her head. "She was standing on the stairs and crying. "She told me..." Vala sucked in a deep breath. "That she was undoing the wrong she had done." She shook her head. "But she spoke of other things too. Of the Rogue, his mother and of something she hid from him." She shook her head. "She would not listen to anything I said." She hesitated. "Anne insisted we must open the burial circle of the Rogue's mother. It was as if a ghost spoke to her."

"There are no such things as ghosts," Giles said softly.

"Nor magic, my Lord," Vala smiled sadly. "Yet there was more. Anne said that the parchment was stolen from the Rogue by his mother and she as much as commanded that we retrieve it." She shuddered. "She was frantic when she spoke."

He gathered her closer as if that would allow him to share her pain.

Vala looked up at him but this time the tears were gone. She wiped her eyes with the back of one hand. "There was more." She dropped her hand. "Parchment, stone, love and love too is three." The last was whispered almost as if she had slipped into a dream.

"She said this?"

"Aye and then, I know not what, if she was pushed or she fell. For the air became thick and heavy and the noise," She hesitated. "The noise Giles was like nothing I had ever heard. I sense it was he, the Rogue. But yet I know not. All I know was that when it was over Anne was dead at the bottom of the stairs."

Giles frowned. "Cecile will not take this well."

"I think in her heart she knew Anne had gone to the other side. It is the second time for her. Her husband left to join the Others."

"She fell to her death?"

"Aye." Vala looked up at him.

Giles released Vala's hand. He strode to where the corpse lay and lifted Anne's body onto a trestle table. "She will be buried with full ceremony before sunset. For now we must find Magna."

Outside the villagers milled just behind where Cynn stood with his legs spread and his thick arms crossed as he blocked the entrance to the keep.

Giles placed a hand on the man's shoulder. "Cynn, make sure that no one enters until I return."

"de Montford, *et tu*!" Turstin shouted.

It was a call to action, to war.

"*Non, si'vous plait!*" Giles shouted. "Stand back! There is nothing we can do here at the moment. Sheath your weapons." Giles walked over to where Turstin and the rest of his men stood. "There has been an accident. Anne died."

"We'll bury the girl," Turstin said. "And Royce after."

"No, you can't," Giles replied. "The girl's mother must direct the burial. Hafne's women would not tolerate otherwise."

"Royce," Vala whispered. Her hand covered her mouth as she looked up at him. "Royce. No!" She shook her head and reached to grasp Giles' arm.

He pulled away from her. "Shelter Royce's body until I return," he said to Turstin. "We'll bury both separately."

"You are right," Turstin agreed and stepped back. "Where is the girl's mother?"

"Still in the village. But there is another matter Vala and I must attend to first."

"Cecile knows," Vala interjected. "She has sensed it, I can feel her grief. She is not here now but she may still try to enter the keep."

"Do not worry, my lady," Turstin reassured.

"Vala?" Her name was a question on Giles' lips.

Silently she took his hand accepting their shared destiny.

●

Come.

"Magna calls us now. We will not find her if we wait," Vala said.

They found Magna at the pond.

"Both Royce's and Anne's death were prophesized. Nothing could have stopped either," Magna said immediately.

"It is not just legend. The Rogue's mother is the ghost of the keep," Vala said.

"You knew that," Magna said shortly.

"She said I was like her."

"You must find the common link and what she has hidden from him." Magna's gaze focused on Giles. "Remember."

She held her staff aloft. "Blood. It is all about bloodlines and it is not. You and Vala, two prestigious lines, two separate bloods." She swept her staff high in the air and smoke plumed in a halo over her head.

And like that she was gone but this time a small white puff of smoke drifted over the forest floor and around them wafted the scent of onion.

"We are related and not by blood. I and many in the village of Ancient blood—and you." Vala tentatively touched his arm.

"Ancient. Of course not." Giles tensed.

"I thought you would say as much. This makes our task more difficult." Vala dropped her hand. "Are you sure? The sight and Ancient blood are clear links."

Giles spanned the air with his hands. "Only Norman."

"Still, even here you can't admit you are Saxon."

"My mother was Saxon," he muttered.

"You are Ancient, Saxon, Norman."

"Nay, I am not Ancient. That is ridiculous."

Vala looked up at him and was unable to hide the startled expression that she knew flitted across her face. How could he not know what she sensed so clearly?

She stood on tiptoe and kissed him. His lips were warm and firm against hers. She deepened the kiss, toying with him. Her hands settled on his shoulders and her lips settled into the kiss.

She couldn't do this.

Abruptly she pushed away from him.

She sighed. The kiss's bitter sweetness still clung achingly familiar on her lips. It was a moment when life, death and desire all collided in one confusing moment.

"You must accept your destiny. You were called and it is time." She pressed her hands against her temples as the answers tumbled like hard stones in a rapid stream.

"I must return. Royce and the woman must be buried." He stalked away.

She sighed softly as his broad back retreated into the distance.

"You too, I know not how, are Ancient," Vala whispered. "As am I," she glanced to the sky where sundogs sparked through the trees. "How else could you be chosen? And how could I not have known sooner?

•

Vala caught up with Giles as he entered the courtyard. And in the keep Giles' men and the villagers both awaited them.

"I told you to remain away," Giles said in a loud voice.

"It was our duty," Edric said. "You would have done no less."

"Done no less?" Giles frowned.

"I know it is tradition for the women to care for the dead. But, with all that has happened they needed help." Edric cleared his throat.

On a pallet laid out on a trestle table was Anne's body, wrapped in clean linen.

"She can't be buried with the others," Esma whispered to Vala. "What shall we do? Surely Cecile will make a fuss if we don't."

But Cecile unexpectedly solved that problem for her as she came up beside them and said, "She must be buried with her father."

"Her father is buried in the clearing that was their camp with the others. We gave what remained a proper burial," Turstin said.

"Thank you," Cecile said. "Anne had a closeness to her father. She'll be buried beside him."

"Cecile, no." Vala reached for Cecile.

Cecile held her hand up. "No, it is what Anne would have wanted. I can only do now what I think would have made her happy."

Deep within the forest, four graves were protected within a circle of stones. Within that circle lay men who had been husbands and fathered children within the village.

Editha marked the sign of the pentagram on Anne's body and laid the shroud of death across her. She glanced to the skies. "The gods have finally called her. Even now she begins her journey."

Cecile choked back a sob as the other women covered the grave. Once the body was covered, the women turned the shovels over to the men. There was no need to remain any longer. Giles and his men would finish and close the circle with the stones that protected good from evil.

•

Giles returned to the keep immediately after burying Anne for Royce still had to be buried. Within the keep on a trestle table he lay wrapped in clean linen with the battle blood washed away. His sword gleamed in the dim light for it was polished to a sheen that would have made his friend proud. Giles swallowed roughly.

Who would have done this? Giles thought.

"He fought for us," a woman said quietly behind him. "He is one of us."

"We have prepared room for him beneath the Trees of Truth," another woman said.

Giles couldn't speak for words would not emerge past the lump in his throat.

Editha took charge. "You." She pointed to Turstin. "And you." She pointed at another of his men. "Place him on the pallet there. We'll carry him now to his burial before the sun sets."

Again they arrived at the burial ground of Hafne. Giles followed the procession being solely directed by the women of Hafne. The grave had already been dug and the shovels rested against one of the trees that circled the small area. The body awaited the final rites.

"Who did this?" Giles whispered to Vala.

"All of us," she replied and rested her hand briefly on his arm.

Giles lifted his friend's body from the pallet and placed him within the grave that the women had dug. He knelt over the grave for a moment and placed the sign of the cross over his forehead before giving Magna room to perform the final rites. Again, the sign of the pentagram was marked on the still forehead. The gossamer veil floated from Magna's hand to settle lightly over Royce's face. Her staff leveled over the grave as she began the chant that offered Royce's soul to his final journey. Sparks flew thick in the air and the thunder cracked as lightning again peeled from the sky. Prayers to the one God merged with prayers to the many. Magna lifted her staff and the thunder and lightning stopped. She slipped away as Giles came forward to drop the first shovel of dirt followed by his men. Each of the Normans dropped a shovel of dirt on their friend.

"He is home," Magna said. "Now you return to yours." She pointed to the keep. "We'll finish here. Here, it is how it is done."

Giles nodded. Behind them the soft whispers of the women and the gentle sound of dirt filling the grave were oddly comforting. For the first time in many days Giles was at peace.

•

Later that night, Vala felt her way along the rocky path to the entrance of the crypt. The full moon was now less than a week away. She shivered from the damp, cool air and the dread of entering the crypt in the pre-dawn dark.

Follow your heart, girl.

The wind kicked up more cold air and twisted harshly around her.

"This damnable wind is nigh ripping the cloth from my back. Where did it come from? There was not even a breeze a minute ago," Giles grumbled.

"The third piece is here. I know it!" Vala moved rapidly along the path.

She squeezed his hand as much to focus her own thoughts as to acknowledge their mission.

His hand trembled and that startled her. "You are afraid."

"I have no fear. The stone trembles. We are on the right path," he said.

"What makes you so sure now?" She was amused considering how skeptical he had been only minutes earlier.

"The crypt's circle will be breached." His voice was devoid of any inflection, matter-of-fact, hollow.

Vala shivered violently.

He gripped her hand tighter and pulled her toward the looming darkness that signaled the entrance to the crypt.

"Aye," she agreed. "The burial circle will be breeched by us."

He released her hand. And despite what he had said only days earlier he asked. "You mean to open the burial circle? Have you taken all leave of your senses? You do not know what is buried there."

"That's not true," Vala replied as they stepped inside the cave.

The light flickered in the chamber. Giles glanced around, staring closely at the symbols that marked the walls. He strode over to the wall and traced a finger along the marks. "Magna says they are older than the Ancients."

The walls around them seemed to vibrate. The symbols pitched and blurred before their eyes.

"A burial ground and the place where he was conceived. Both are the same," Giles said.

The world seemed to spin as the words echoed in the silent void as if something waited with baited breath.

"The inner circle protects the crypt," Vala said.

Vala bent down and lifted a stone, then two, until there was space to walk within the gap. Once inside, she did the same to the second circle. Around them the air was alive with vibration. The whispers of the Ancients seemed to intensify so that the voices blended and masked in a continual vibration of sound.

She stepped inside the circle. "She's buried here. His mother." She stepped in awe within the circle.

She brushed her fingers lightly along the stones that covered the floor. "The other piece of the parchment is here. You can feel the vibration on the earth. Here, place your hand there," Vala directed. "Do you feel it?" she breathed.

The whispers around them rose in volume.

"Is it wise to open the circle like we have?"

"But the remainder of the parchment is here. Grave or not, it is right. How can it be any more right when its occupant has commanded it?"

The sand was hardened, crystallized by the damp, salt and age. Grains of sand gouged her fingers and ripped her nails. Yet it gave easier than ground undisturbed for ages should.

"Here it is." Vala pulled the thin, partially rotted vellum from the shallow grave and waved it triumphantly.

The air around them came alive with sound, warm rustlings, words unidentified.

"The Rogue's mother stole it from him and hid it in her crypt," Vala said.

"She is a spirit. How could she?"

"She couldn't, but someone else could," Vala said with surety as what she had only guessed before became a realization. "The ghost could use trickery. The same one who betrayed Hafne's women and gave him a piece of the parchment."

"Anne. You think Anne did this?"

"Why else did Anne return to the keep that day when all the villagers ran?" She rocked back on her heels. "There were many things that happened that day," Vala replied softly. "Royce and Anne both lost their lives."

"Tell me of Anne. You think she took the parchment. Why?"

"Why else did she seek out the ghost the day she died? Why else did the ghost speak to her? It was Anne, Giles. I am sure of it. Somehow she stole the parchment back from the Rogue. And following the ghost's directions she buried the parchment in the crypt where the ghost knew the Rogue couldn't reach once the circle was closed."

The voices that had been long silent began to sing softly in the thick blackness of the far reaches of the keep.

The One.

"The One," he repeated. His voice was a whisper that melted into the dark recesses.

"Giles?"

The One. The One.

"Enough!" Vala screamed into the darkness. "Stop it! Just stop it!" She dropped to the floor and covered her face with her hands. It was too much.

He stroked her shoulders and then drew her to him.

"Admit what you are," she said fiercely. "You must."

"Vala," he whispered. "Sweet Vala, I can't."

"When?"

"Soon," he replied as his head dipped.

She tilted her head up as his came down and his mouth opened over hers. She drank him in, greedily, without thought, her body curving to his. His arms wrapped around her and pulled her tighter. It felt right. It just was. Before, their joining had been about power, passion and what she believed must be. This time it was what she wanted. There was nothing else. Her heart beat a rough dance against her ribs as she melted into him and he into her.

His lips seared hers.

There was nothing gentle in the kiss.

Fiery kisses awoke velvety skin.

Hands skimmed and brushed erotically, touching everywhere, nothing forbidden.

Someone groaned.

Hands lifted seductively through hair, tremors skimmed goose bumps against overheated skin.

They slid to the ground. The shock of the cold rock only added an edge to the play, to skin already alight with sensation.

Their joining was a rough, passionate dance where there was little give and considerable take from both.

The shadows danced and from somewhere deep in the bowls

of the cave an entity screamed as the two lay in the aftermath of their passion, the sacred circle stained with the scent of sex and something else. Something that Vala had fought with for so long. She loved him.

Chapter Twenty-five

She loved him and the reality caused her hands to tremble. It was too much. It was too soon and she had no idea what to do with the knowledge. "We must leave—now." Vala rose gracefully to her feet and pulled her tunic over her head. "We're not alone."

The light sputtered as the torch danced thinly in the icy breeze that dashed through the cave.

The chill air was beginning to warm and the sun was rising as Vala and Giles burst from the small opening and drank in the first welcome breaths of sea-salted air.

"The pond," they both said. Together they changed direction, walking quickly away from the keep with the piece of parchment clutched in Vala's hand.

At the pond the placid water beckoned and for a moment Vala only wanted to slip into the peaceful depths. "Magna put both pieces away where they couldn't be reached by him, the Rogue." It was so much easier to focus on the prophecy for it was so much more immediate and so much less troubling than the emotion that broiled so close to the surface.

Love.

She knew naught what to do with it. She couldn't love him. And nay, she could never tell him. "Part of the long ago legend is that the seer's stone was removed from the cliff beneath where one lone Tree of Truth has grown for as long as the Ancients have existed. It was when Hafne began that the seer's stone came to reside in the pond. That is where Magna has placed the remaining two pieces." She pointed without looking at him. "Within the cliff. There can be no other place."

"The sight?"

"Aye," she agreed as she admitted what made that statement such a surety.

They climbed up the cliff by following a narrow path that led to a small crevice. Above the crevice a knotted, worn lone Tree of Truth grew. Its lime green branches hung low over the cliff as if by its age alone it had lost the will to pull its leaves toward the sky.

Vala reached into a crack in the cliff beneath the tree and her fingers slipped across moss. She peered in. "There's nothing." Then, she brushed against something smooth, dry, a roll of parchment.

"Do you have it?" Giles asked, leaning over her shoulder so that as she pulled back they almost tumbled.

"Is it both?"

"I don't know," she replied as they climbed down the cliff. By the pond, she squatted back on her heels. Together they bent over the rolled parchment.

He reached over and fingered the parchment. He held out his hand. She gave him the parchment. He unrolled the two fragile pieces, their surfaces mutating from rough to smooth, golden to plain even before they were open. She placed the third piece beside the two pieces of parchment. They fit one against the other and despite the burns and tearing they made a perfect whole.

"I can make no sense of this," Giles said. "Do you think Magna would be able to read this?"

Vala shook her head. "We, not the Ancients, must find the answer."

Vala leaned over the pieces. The pieces glowed and meshed. She squinted and leaned closer.

"Do you see it?" she asked.

"Aye." Amazement edged his voice as for the first time they were able to read the prophecy.

Sweet love
Stones United
Stones Returned

"Sweet love," Vala said. "A lover?" She shivered.

"Nay," Giles replied shaking his head. "It speaks of innocence."

"Stones united, stones returned," he read the next lines. "That seems fairly easy to understand. We must unite the stones and return them. Return them where?"

"To the pond from which Mervaine first raised the original seer's stone," Vala said.

"The writing has become indecipherable."

Vala looked at him sharply.

"It is very clear," she said softly. "I'll read what it says to you."

Long ago in a time before time there lived a people.

Giles listened as Vala read the story of the Ancients' including the creation of the Rogue and the beginning of the prophecy. It was a story he had heard many times before. A story that was now as real to him as breathing. He listened raptly, mesmerized by her clear voice. The sweet alto swirled around him. He had to force himself to focus on her words, the text and what it meant. His eyes followed the strange words on the parchment as she read them. And as he did the words began to become clear as if they were translated as they read, from a strange language to something clear and more understandable to him than any other language, Norman French. He shook his head like a dog emerging from the river with a stick.

"You speak French," he said thickly.

The manuscript dropped from her fingers. It was only his quick reaction, warrior sharp that prevented the fragile parchment from dropping to the ground.

"Vala," he said sharply, "what is the matter?"

He placed the parchment back in her hands. Now the story she read was their own from the birth of Rosaline's babe, to his arrival, the death of the Others, Royce, everything that had happened here so far she read from the manuscript.

He grabbed the parchment from her hands. "You're making this up!" he snarled. "That is not written here." The paper swirled in front of him. Big trembling symbols that made no sense and then the words became clear even to him.

The Norman watches Vala while she sleeps. Often he asks himself, will she too, like his mother, leave him?

Giles dropped the parchment and cursed. The thing knew his inner most thoughts. He drew back, realizing in that moment what it felt to be violated.

"Giles, what did you see?"

"Nothing," he snapped.

"That is not true," she said softly and picked the parchment up. "It is unclear again. Now there is nothing but yet before our lives were mapped on this page. It is magical, yet still has not told us how this ends."

"Maybe we do not want to know," Giles replied but he lifted the parchment from her hands and willed his fingers not to tremble.

Monti for you we have long awaited. A mother of the chosen, one with Ancient blood can never stay. She returns when the Ancients call. A male, blood of the three, the Ancients rejoiced from the time of your birth til your return to Hafne. You have been hidden from he that was banished, til now, beware.

"By the Saints holy bones," Giles breathed and the parchment slipped from his fingers.

"Giles?" Vala reached for him.

He pulled away. His throat worked convulsively and he glanced away.

"What is it?"

"Monti," he replied thickly. "Magna called me Monti as a small boy. She meant to leave."

"Magna?" Vala asked confused.

"My mother." His throat worked again and he turned to face her. He wiped the back of his hand across his eyes. "My mother was part Ancient but she was also Saxon." He glanced with a half smile at Vala. "My father was Norman. But you knew that."

"What else?"

"Nothing." He reached for the aged paper. "Nothing."

He was right—not even the original words remained. It was empty.

"We must write the end ourselves," she said.

"What of the verse?"

Vala reached for his hand, "We shall mull it over as we write our destiny."

Vala fingered the ring. "Tis been with relatives too far back to count. My mother most recently and before that my grandmother." She met his gaze full on and he almost rocked back at the pain he saw there. "Both were doomed by love."

"Vala," he began.

"Nay." She held up her hand against him even as she stood up. "I am fine. Let us go back."

They walked toward the keep in silence. As they emerged from the forest she grasped his arm. "We must unite the stones soon."

"He has the second."

"Yes, deep within the third tower."

"A tower that is no longer accessible or even visible," Giles replied.

"True," Vala replied. "But he wants me. He calls for me to come. Maybe if—"

"No! You will not," Giles threw off her hand and grasped her shoulders, drawing her back, away from him, so that he could meet her eyes. "No." He shook her slightly. "Do not go when he calls. We must go together. When the time is right. It is the only way. Promise me."

"I can't."

•

He could taste it. After all the lonely eons, success was close. His heir was so near he had almost touched her on a number of occasions. One piece of the parchment was safe from those who would destroy him and one half of the seer's stone in his possession. Stone, parchment, heir, Hafne would soon be his!

Now he rolled the stone between his fingers and stared at the creature, "Ewaldo, return the second half of the seer's stone to me. Go!"

It was not until later that night that he discovered what she had done. When he lifted the golden stone that held the piece of the parchment and discovered it was gone. His roar of anguish pierced every corner of the keep.

Chapter Twenty-six

The Norman slept as if there was no threat. Ewaldo worked quickly for the potion he had placed in his ale would not last long. He pulled the eating knife from beneath the Norman's tunic. The Norman began to snore.

His pouch.

The words of his master were snarled and impatient this eventide.

The Norman shifted in his sleep. Ewaldo did not breathe for he was scared that any movement would arouse him. Still, there was nothing and he lifted the tunic looking for the pouch that held the stone.

His knife sliced through the leather thong and he freed it.

He must leave now and return to the master. But even as he thought this, he was drawn to the man on the bed, his body so big, so rich, so full of blood, of life. It made death so much more exciting.

The knife skimmed easily through flesh. The warm blood pulsed across his hands. Life, blood, death. He so craved death.

Return to me. The voice was a roar of wind in his ears. He ran for the window to climb down the vines that grew up the wall, exactly the way he had arrived.

•

"Vala." The voice spoke softly but reached deep into her consciousness.

"What?" She muttered as she came awake. Threads of sleep still tangled her thoughts.

Magna thrust a pouch at Vala.

"He'll die without you," Magna stated flatly, her black eyes sparking in the dim light.

Sleep fled and she knew Magna referred to Giles.

He can't die. Please no, Vala prayed as her feet fairly flew over the dark earth.

Vala entered the keep and was immediately assaulted by a roar of men's voices. The fire burned cheerfully, the dogs slept and the men bantered back and forth. What were they doing, joking when Giles lay dying somewhere in this very keep?

"Where is Giles?"

Vala ran for the stairs without waiting for a reply. Her heart pounded in her throat and it was difficult to catch her breath.

Upstairs, Giles lay on the bed. Blood pulsed from his wrist into a pool onto the floor.

Vala rushed to his side.

"I should never have left you," she murmured as she regretted her decision to leave the keep and return to her hut. It had been selfish. She had been thinking only of her own need to avoid him and to dodge the desire. To put up a wall between them for he would never love her. But now none of that mattered. Her fingers shook and she took a deep breath. This was no time for emotion. Giles needed her.

He can't die. It was only in that moment that she truly began to realize what he meant to her. He couldn't die for she didn't know when it had happened but he had become everything. She needed him. But his face was shadowed, death hovered closely.

Another voice called.

"Nay Giles, I love you," she whispered. But the man that lay on the bed was silent as he hovered between light and the final darkness.

Vala, do not deny me. The voice was strong, deep, with the sureness that only age brings. *Come to me.*

Vala stopped. Her soul was torn. She took one step toward the door before realizing what she did. "Nay!"

Shaking, she returned to Giles. She picked up the injured arm and pushed her fingers against the wound, temporarily staying the flow of blood.

"Place your fingers here," she instructed Turstin, who had just entered the room. She began to stitch as Giles' blood pulsed between her fingers. When she was finished she rose, ran her finger down his cheek.

"He'll sleep." Vala gathered up her healing instruments. Even with Turstin still in the room she dropped a light kiss on Giles' whisker-rough cheek. There was naught else she could do except pray to the gods and offer up the love she had never offered him.

•

Come.

Ewaldo trembled. He slid into the shadows of the great hall and watched.

The girl, Vala, appeared. She moved silently. He imagined the sweet blood that pulsed beneath that pale skin and licked his lips.

Kill her and you will never die.

It was the ultimate threat for all he wanted all these endless eons was death and it was all he couldn't have.

Return!

Ewaldo covered his ears. His hands began to shake.

I can help. The voice was so different from the other, warm and full of hope.

He started and blinked as he focused on another beautiful, pale skinned girl. But this was one was dark haired. He reached eagerly for her, imagining how her white flesh would feel and stumbled as the vision disappeared. Instead an old woman leaned against the wall with a sage smile on her face.

You can still smell the blood.

"Aye." The words came out in a throaty whisper. She placed her palms over his hands, cupping them between her own. Oddly, the bloodlust disappeared.

"What do you want?" The words choked from his closed throat.

I want the stone and for that I'll free you.

"From him, the Rogue?"

The hag slowly shook her head.

From this life.

He whirled on her. "How did you know?" The stone heated in his hand and a wind howled around him. Panicked, he dropped the stone.

He is not the only one who can release you. Let me.

Something stroked his cheek, a caress. A tear formed in his eye. He touched the moisture with wonder. He had never cried.

Come to me. The command was laced with honey and came from the third tower.

"Take me," he whispered facing the place where the woman had stood and tears rolled down his cheeks.

The aged, gnarled little woman appeared before him briefly, beckoning and then the wind returned howling and sucked the essence from him. He vanished like he never existed.

In the corner of the keep, purple light shafted as half of the seer's stone was freed. The stone lay where it had been dropped. A scorched circle ringed where it lay.

•

"You are awake." Relief rushed through Vala as she pulled the coverlet around Giles.

"How long has it been?" Giles asked and pushed the coverlet back.

"You have been like this for two days. In the beginning we did not think you would live."

"Much has happened?" he asked slowly.

"Aye. The seer's stone is gone." But the stone, the prophecy—none of it mattered. Only that Giles was awake and that he lived.

"My stone was stolen? The Rogue?"

"Nay, one of the Others. The only one remaining." She ran her finger along the stitches that bit into his wrist. "I'll take these out in a day."

"You saved my life." He shifted to face her. "Who is this of which you speak?"

The smell of onions was overpowering.

"He was special to him in a way that you do not want to know," Magna said.

"Who is he?"

"Look for the missing stone. It is here." And with that she was again gone.

Giles tried to raise himself up but sweat popped on his forehead.

Vala gently pushed him back. "Let me. Now that you are awake I'll search."

"No," Giles whispered taking her hand and drawing him to her.

"Tis too dangerous. Vala, I can't bear if you are hurt." His voice became weaker and his eyes closed.

Vala clung to his hand. He was a strong man and never had she seen him so vulnerable. She couldn't leave him. For now she was his strength. She sat with him, holding his hand until his breath evened out and he slept.

"Vala," a woman's voice called softly. "Vala." The door opened slightly.

"Come in, Esma," Vala replied.

Esma opened the door tentatively, her hair askew and her eyes wide.

Her hands were bathed in a soft purple shadow.

Esma held her hand out and Vala gasped.

"I found it in a corner of the hall."

"What does this mean?"

"The creature is dead. The one they called Ewaldo," Esma whispered. "There is nothing left but ashes. I watched Magna take him."

"And you told me not?" Vala frowned.

"I did not want to concern you, not when Lord Giles hovered between life and death."

Vala took the stone from Esma. "It will be over soon."

"I'll leave you for now," Esma whispered.

Vala nodded. She fingered the stone as Esma quietly slipped from the room. With Giles asleep, she was alone. Had not the parchment said the two halves of the seer's stone must be returned together? By the time Giles awoke she would have the second stone and they could return them to the pond. And that would be that— the curse ended.

Vala, my love, come to me.

He was weak. The energy he had gotten from the Others gone. The Rogue needed another life or he must kill to get energy. She shivered. The knowledge was clear and unbidden.

"Nay?" she whispered shaking her head violently. "This must end."

Come to me.

The voice was faint and so very familiar. For a moment Vala forgot the stone. She ached deep inside to go to that voice.

The stench of onion was overpowering.

Magna appeared briefly. "Nay Vala."

The scent of roses filled her nostrils, the smell of onions gone.

Vala dragged in a trembling whiff. She had not smelled roses since she was a small girl. Before they arrived in Hafne. Roses had been her mother's favorite scent. Jars of rose water her favorite concoction, her cure-all for most everything. Roses to Vala were the essence of her mother.

Vala.

The voice had the gentle, fluted tone of her mother. *You will not get another chance.* The voice, still so like her mother's but strained.

She glided quietly through the hall, skirting the smoke clotted room where men diced and the steward regaled them all with a yarn. Silently Vala went to the hidden door in the back of the keep. It was open but a velvety fog skirted the ground and hid the path.

Vala stopped. The mysterious pull was weak now as the fog lifted from the ground and a shaft of purple skittered along and stopped at Vala's feet.

"By the Saints!" The second stone she had come for now lay at her feet like a gift.

Vala reached for the stone and drew back.

The stone gleamed. Shafts shot through the air and stained her tunic with purple light. The stone rolled away. Vala followed. She reached down, surely it would not be a difficult thing to just pick it up and run. The stone rolled farther away.

Vala followed it.

The stone stopped.

She reached down. Touched it.

The stone was velvety warm, like something alive. Then it slipped from under her fingers and rolled away.

And so it went for what seemed like forever. Then from nowhere, a ladder dropped slowly down through the misted glow. The stone began to rise. Each time Vala reached for it, it faded into nothing.

"This is not right," Vala thought. The thought felt heavy, syrupy. The smell of roses surrounded her. And her feet took her where the stone led.

Like a dream she climbed the ladder. The gold rungs were warm in her hands, and above, the third tower glowed.

The stone was gone when Vala reached the top of the ladder. The tower was the same as it had been that day with Giles, the same, but not. It felt so much emptier. The birds did not sing, the

Grechners were absent and the scent of honey was not there.

The scent of roses was gone. Her mother was not here. Never had been.

Of course not. She is dead. The voice was pleasant enough.

He hovered above her, his black robes swirling seductively.

Do you know who I am?

Wulfgar!

As if he read her thoughts, the face no longer appeared like Wulfgar's. Instead a handsome, Saxon warrior, a young man, beautiful, angelic peered out from beneath the hood of his robe.

"Who are you?" Vala whispered and was terrified of the answer.

The figure floated and then vanished but his presence lay deep within the room.

He reappeared, smiled and crooked his finger. *Blood of my blood.* Again, his image began to fade. *You too are Ancient. You belong with me.*

In his translucent hand she could see the flash of purple. The stone. Her gaze shot back to him. She would incite his anger; he would forget he held the stone. "You are nothing! You are evil and the Ancients will destroy you."

"Destroy me!"

"Destroy you," Vala repeated and then leaned forward. "For you couldn't even destroy your own mother. She still lives," she said triumphantly.

He spun. He disappeared and the stone hovered in the air held by the unseen hand. The stone dropped and shattered, and purple shards fell everywhere.

"Vala," the voice called and a gray vortex began to swirl.

"Vala." Other voices called.

Aedre, Willa, and Esma appeared at the top of the ladder and Editha behind them.

"Vala, run!" Esma screamed.

"I can't," Vala said calmly. "I must choose."

"The runes say it isn't time," Willa's voice shook.

The Rogue drifted toward the women. "The women of Hafne," he purred.

The stench of rot was almost overpowering.

"It is our power that will end him," Editha said firmly. "Join hands."

They reached for Vala.

Vala.

The scent of honey was sweet and sticky, and laced with the scent of roses.

"Nay," she whispered and held her hand out to the women.

You belong with me. Love.

"Hurry, Vala. He speaks of love. Hurry before it is too late." Esma urged.

"Love will break the curse."

Tentatively she reached out and his robe grazed her fingers.

You are mine.

"Nay!" She dropped her hand.

The Rogue spun away and as he went the purple shards gathered and collected, returning back to the solid half of the seer's stone.

"Vala," Esma's said urgently. Her aura and those of the other women reached for Vala, wrapped around her. Vala reached and clasped Esma's hand.

Their energy filled the room. Together their auras hummed.

No!

The stone skipped across the floor.

Vala dove for it and scrambled for the ladder where she followed the others to the ground and ran. Behind them the third tower slowly faded into the mist and disappeared.

Chapter Twenty-seven

The water was a blue so deep that no light penetrated the surface. Instead the warm sunlight skidded across the surface and threw deep shadows on the surrounding rocks.

Vala and Giles held hands—and each held a stone.

"Ready?" she asked.

He nodded and the strong planes of his face were real and comforting. Gone was the weakness as surely as the stitches she had only removed this morning.

They each pitched their stone high into the air over the pond. Both stones hovered in the air, bathing their amethyst glow over the water. The sandy bottom was clear in their glow and then they fell. They slid through the surface without even a ripple.

"It isn't over." Giles fingered the empty pouch at his waist.

"It is a start."

"It was too simple." He turned to her and drew her into his arms. "I can't begin to tell you how grateful I am."

She laid her head against his shoulder. "You could try."

He chuckled and his hand stroked her hair, free again from the wimple. She sighed against his shoulder and gave herself to his caress.

"Vala, you are my undoing. I know naught if I am coming or going around you."

She raised her head, her hands on his shoulders, his mouth only a heartbeat away. "'Tis a good thing," she questioned. "For I feel the same."

"Truly?"

"Truly."

Overhead screeching broke through their thoughts.

"What was that?" Giles asked as his strong hands continued to hold her shoulders.

"Do you think we have missed something? Is there something else we needed to do?" She asked as she looked up at him and the Grechners called from the trees.

"I do not know, sweet Vala," he said as he leaned down and kissed her.

"There is no more we can do this day," she said when the kiss ended.

"Except this," he said as he pulled her to him and kissed her again.

•

Fools! The gray hair danced around Magna's head. The cane swung in the air. They had waited for hours to undue the damage.

As the sun faded, Mervaine's staff rested on the surface of the water and Magna circled, her feet stepping delicately between air and water, her staff flagging the air. Behind them, beneath the Trees of Truth, the Ancients watched and waited. Mervaine began to chant.

The water churned and spun red as violet shards lapped the shores. The Grechners shrieked. The stones lifted through the oblique waters. They hovered in the air around the Ancients before dropping into Mervaine's hands.

He shook his head gently as he glanced at the stones. Sliding across the water he stood in front of Magna. "I charge you with their return."

"As always, my love, I accept." Magna reached for the stones and slid them deep into the folds of her velvet gown.

•

The next day the women gathered, all the women of Hafne and two Norman men, Robert and Turstin.

"Why are they here?" Cecile snapped as soon as she saw the two Normans. "This has nothing to do with them."

"I disagree," Turstin replied. "This is now our home as well as it is yours."

Aedra stood beside Turstin. "He is right, we must learn to live with the Normans."

"The stones have been returned," Esma said.

"Aye," Editha said. "The stones have been removed from the

pond by Magna. She has entrusted me with their care."

"You?" Turstin asked.

"That is our first task," Editha replied. "We'll hide the stones, safeguard them until Giles and Vala are ready to act. They returned them to the pond too soon. And they can't read the parchment, not fully, not without us," Editha said.

"We must make our support known," Aedre replied.

"But first we must safeguard the stones," Editha replied.

"The crypt," Cecile said.

"It is the one of two places where the Rogue can't reach. His power exceeds all that he has known before. He can reach deep into our thoughts, find where we have hidden them but he can't reach there. We must go now before he has a chance to act against us," Editha agreed.

"I'll lead," Esma said. "I go there every day to light the torch." She pulled a rope from around her neck where the holy relic dangled. "I have this to protect me. What of the rest of you?"

Editha held up the small pentagram that dangled around her neck. Cecile spat and said she did not need any luck charm. Another carried a pinch of salt and so it went. Each woman protected by their own beliefs and the customs of the land.

"Is there naught but superstition on this land?" Robert whispered to Turstin.

"Tis not superstition," Turstin whispered back. He reached into his tunic and pulled out a Christian cross.

"Jesu! Tis like a plague," Robert muttered. "I have nothing. Do you think I need it?"

"You must believe in something," Turstin said. "That is what will protect you."

"I'll pray."

The evening shadows found them taking the same treacherous path that Vala and Giles had traversed twice in the last little while. The moon gave only glimpses of the path but fortunately it was not fully dark.

The stones burned hot in the pouch around Editha's neck. The once dark path was now lit by the faint mauve sheen of the stones. They entered the cave led by Esma, who lifted the torch from its holder.

"I have never gone farther than this spot," Esma whispered.

"Let me," said Aedre.

"No," Turstin took the torch. "I'll lead."

"Listen. Already our strength has increased," Editha said. "The whispers are silent."

They followed the torchlight as Turstin led them deep into the cave directly below the keep where the crypt lay. There they rolled the stones of the outer circle away and then opened the inner circle. Turstin reached for his eating dagger.

"There is no need to bury them," Editha said. "Place the stones in the center. They will be fine as long as both circles are closed."

"When the sun has risen five times, we'll return," Editha said.

"We are safe for now," Esma breathed as they left the crypt.

"Maybe," Editha whispered darkly, "but in two score years on this earth I have seen much. Beware."

Chapter Twenty-eight

Within the tower he paced. Vala was moving away from him. He could feel the thin ties slowly slipping away. He must have some of his power returned. With the energy of the Others gone, he was weak. He needed energy. Even borrowed. He slipped from the tower room, snarling as he glided toward the village.

Come to me. The Rogue called softly. He knew that the weakest would come shortly.

•

In the morning, the women discovered Cecile was gone. There had been no sound, no warning. Only Cecile's daughter, Sibley, was curled fast asleep alone by the hearth.

"Cecile was called by him last night," Editha said with a surety.

"She is in the land of the ancestors," Magna replied.

"And Sibley has no one." Editha held up her hands. "Now what?"

"Sibley has you," Magna told her.

"There is nothing I can do for the child," Editha said sadly. "I have raised all the children I will have for this lifetime."

Magna stopped stirring the pot over which she always seemed to be hovering. "There are many things you can do for the child. The gods have spoken. Yet again you are a mother. You have no choice."

•

"Will the death never end?" Vala whispered as she lay on her back in the clearing by the pond. The clouds were only beginning to gather. It would rain this day, in the afternoon, as it always did. As always the rain would provide no moisture for any of the inhabitants of Hafne. The rain of death as Vala had begun to think of it.

She snuggled closer to Giles for comfort, to still the thoughts, for the eroticism of his bare skin on hers.

"What are you thinking?" He grumbled as he traced an idle thumb along her breast.

She glanced over at him. His face was marred by streaks of sunlight that tangled amidst the leaves of the ancient oak. "I was thinking I would miss this." *And that I love you.* But the words wouldn't come, not yet.

"Are you going somewhere?"

"Nay but someday you will marry and then ..."

"And then what? I will not be without you, Vala." His thumb traced her stiffening nipple. One leg lay across her legs, warm, comforting, arousing. A foot grazed hers and slowly began to stroke her ankle. She squirmed.

"Then, this will end."

"I have asked you to wed." His lips followed his thumb, and he rained gentle kisses before rising to look at her.

She looked deep in his eyes searching for the answer she needed, for the love for which he would not speak. But it was not just unrequited love that made her hesitate, what resided in the tower, the Rogue, called to her and he wouldn't stop. Something drew her to him and even Magna was silent on the matter. Vala did not know if she had the strength to resist.

"You were thinking of love, too," Giles said.

She started.

"Your thoughts shout in the silence." His lips closed over hers and his body pressed against hers.

Caught in the fog of desire, Vala was blind to all else. Only later did she remember the distant rumble of wooden wheels that her conscience had so effectively hidden from her. Only later, did she learn that outside their lair within the woods, the world they knew was on the precipice of change. For now, all that mattered was the feel of her body imprinted on his.

•

Vala entered the bailey behind the visitors. She had stayed after Giles had left the pond and savored the last minute of peace. Already the men who had accompanied the party had dismounted. She skirted around the cart and stopped.

Something was not right. Love flooded her. Vala almost choked on the richness of the feeling. *Giles*. But the feeling she had so long awaited was not directed at her. She turned to the cart where the heavily pregnant woman was being helped down.

"Mathilde!" Giles' shouted and sprinted toward the woman. "I can't believe it is you." He gathered her in his arms and swung her around. "I did not recognize you."

"I should say not." The woman laughed softly. "I have grown much."

Vala couldn't believe her eyes. The man who had taken her literally only moments before now held another in his arms. And a woman so obviously pregnant that only dread could register in the pit of Vala's stomach.

"I missed you, love," the woman said as Giles placed her carefully on her feet.

"Show me this new holding of yours."

He glanced at the keep. "My new holding." He glanced down at her belly. "But first you must rest."

Vala hurried over. "I'm Vala. Welcome."

"Thank you." The woman nodded slightly before returning her attention to Giles.

Obviously dismissed, Vala shrugged and turned to the carriage and driver. She took a few steps and almost collided with Robert. She gave him a half smile and turned back to where Giles stood with the mystery woman.

"Who is she to you?" the woman asked as if Vala weren't nearby.

Vala moved closer, curious as to what he would say and what it might reveal about their visitor.

"The village birther," Giles replied.

"Giles?" And in that one word Vala demanded he say more. She was not just a birther, not to him. She knew from his look, the narrowed eyes and the slightly sheepish tilt to his mouth that he was not going to offer more.

The woman whispered in a knowing voice that carried, "She calls you Giles, not Lord de Montford."

"The women here are like no other."

Within hours he moved the woman to his bedchamber, and confused, Vala went to the stable. Merva shoved her muzzle into

Vala's shoulder.

"Ahh, girl. Things are easier for you. You have chosen Ramion and he, you. There is no other. For me, it is not so simple," she said.

"She's missed you."

Vala shivered at the sound of Giles' voice.

"I had thought more of you," she whispered. "You could have been honest in the beginning. I knew naught of Mathilde's existence."

"T'was a shock for me, too," Giles agreed. "But now I can only take care of her; she has no one." He laid a hand on the mare's neck. "You understand, do you not? Mathilde isn't like you. She's not strong. She can't survive alone."

"She's due any day."

"Aye, and I rely on you to help her. Will you not?"

"I refuse no woman my birthing skills." Vala held back all the anger and regret as she willed him to explain, to offer a reasonable explanation.

"She is my dear friend's widow. She is like a sister to me." He took her hand and pulled her gently to her feet. "You would think that after all that has come between us?"

"Why have you not explained sooner?" Vala's heart skipped a beat. "I thought it was your babe."

He nodded grimly. "I'd thought you would trust more."

"Lord Giles!" The squire Ainsley stood in the stable doorway. "My Lord. The woman, Mathilde, she is calling for you."

"We'll talk later." Giles touched her arm briefly.

"Mayhap," Vala agreed. But with night trickling in, hope seemed thinner than it had earlier in the day.

•

Later that night snores echoed through the hall. The cool spring air chilled the thin blanket. Rather than lying awake and shivering Vala rose from her pallet.

"Where are you going?" Esma whispered into the darkness.

"Shhh, go back to sleep."

Outside the breeze was brisk and Vala pulled her cloak tighter around her. The third tower was visible tonight, lit by something far brighter than torchlight. The light winked and then was dark. Only the silhouette of the two towers remained.

Daughter. The voice was stronger, surer and hauntingly familiar.

To belong again, to know love was a powerful lure and Vala's heart pulled toward the voice. "Nay," she whispered. She began to turn away, then stopped. Behind her the tower was again bathing everything in its path in light. A shadow swept by the open window and then was gone.

Her heart pounded.

Come to me. My child, my love.

The words were like warm treacle and even knowing their deception she was tempted. "Father," she whispered, testing the sound of the word on her lips. "Nay! My father is dead." And this time, even her fieriest attempt was not enough to make her believe those words. And it was many hours before she returned to her pallet. Where for a time she slept until hands shook her gently and she opened her eyes to see Giles.

"Vala, I need you."

"Mathilde?"

"Aye," he said as panic made his voice rougher than normal. "Get up, please. I fear there is trouble."

"The babe is full term and daylight is near." Vala sat up.

"There is something else you must know, Edward was Norman and Mathilde Saxon and she knows not else."

"Giles, is it possible—a babe, blood of the three?"

He took her hand and pulled her gently to her feet. "Hurry."

In the bedchamber, the fire roared and the heat was overwhelming. Vala pulled the fur coverlet from the bed. "Do not put another stick of wood on that fire."

"I was told that heat eased the humors and took some of the pain." Giles shrugged.

"You? Since when do men know such things?"

"I," he swallowed. "T'was many years ago."

Vala felt the memory flash through his mind and she jerked as it jarred him with forgotten intensity.

"I am surprised either lived."

"The babe did not," Giles said softly.

"The woman?"

"She was my mother. I am sorry. I can do many things. But I cannot do this."

"Tis fine Giles. This is what I do."

Their eyes met and locked across the room. Vala sucked in her breath at what she saw there. Trust and something else, something deeper and truer but before she could grasp what it meant, it was gone.

"*Merci, mon amour.*"

The door shut on his last words.

•

The woman had been in labor for hours. Already she was weak. Vala returned to the village for her birthing basket.

"It is too late."

Magna appeared beside her.

"Where have you been?"

But Magna had disappeared again. *It is not your fault.*

"Not my fault." Vala shook her head. There had been much death. As the birther she should bring life not death. Maybe with this babe she could redeem herself.

The great door swung heavily behind her, the thud only partially masking Magna's whispered words. *This, too, is prophesized.*

"What is not?" Vala snapped. "Maybe this time I'll change your blessed prophecy."

In the room, she set her basket down and went immediately to where Mathilde lay. Vala pulled the cover back. She gasped at what she saw. A tiny foot showed. Nay, this was worse than she thought. "Mathilde." The woman's name felt foreign on her lips. "Your babe needs some help but I can't promise that it will not hurt."

The woman's eyes were glazed. "Do it," she murmured and her lips barely moved.

Vala gave Mathilde a tea steeped with willow meant to ease the pain. She rinsed her hand and arm with warm water heated over the fire. Within the water were peppermint and other cleansing herbs to remove the bad humors. She returned to Mathilde. "Now, breathe in a deep breath and cling to this." She handed her a thick piece of cloth. "Deep breath," she instructed and pushed into Mathilde's womb. Mathilde screamed as Vala pushed past the small foot and hand and felt the body of a babe, and then another.

"Twins," she breathed.

Sweat glistened on Mathilde's brow and her face was drained of all color.

"Mathilde," Vala said with urgent desperation. "Mathilde!" She raised her voice trying to reach the woman before she slipped into unconsciousness and eventually to the land of the Ancestors. "Stay with me, please," she begged.

"Hurry," Mathilde said faintly and her eyes closed.

With the babes finally in position, Vala again turned her attention back to Mathilde. Praying the woman had enough strength to birth the babes quickly.

"Matilda," Vala called.

Nothing. Mathilde's belly quivered with a contraction. Her eyes were closed.

Vala sucked in a gasp as Mathilde's aura disappeared.

"Nay!" Vala cried as the aura flickered and returned, sparking faintly around the woman. Another contraction disturbed the taut skin and Mathilde groaned and opened her eyes.

"I am so thirsty." Her words were faint but her aura was stronger.

Vala gave her a sip of tea. "Take some deep breaths for there is work yet for you to do."

"It was too soon," Mathilde murmured. "Edward sent me back. The babes yet need me."

"That they do," Vala said firmly. "For many years."

"Nay, for now."

A contraction rocked her and she clutched Vala's arm. Mercifully with one babe in position that birth was quick. A girl.

Vala wiped the birth matter from the small body. The babe let out a tiny cry. Vala wrapped the babe in the worn cloth that she had warmed by the fire and placed the babe beside her mother. Mathilde could do no more than glance at the child before another contraction rocked her.

"You can do it, Mathilde. You must. Just a little longer."

"I can't birth another," Mathilde panted. "You and Giles will take the babe. He loves you."

"There is no truth in that. You will keep your babe, both of them."

"Nay, Vala. You are wrong."

•

They buried one of the babes that morn—a boy child born with the shroud of death long on him. And again in so few days Magna raised her staff to the heavens and offered the tiny body to the gods.

Cynn crossed himself and wiped a tear that trailed down his cheek. "Always the babes," he muttered. "When will it stop?"

"Soon, I hope," Vala said as they left the burial ground together. "I do not think any of us can endure much more death."

"At least there is the other babe," Cynn said dolefully. "A girl," he said glumly. Then brightened. "The first live birth this year. Mayhap the curse has weakened."

"Mayhap," Vala said and knew that something was still very wrong. Despite returning the stones to the pond, the curse had not ended. The Rogue still lived.

Troubled, she left Cynn far behind as she hurried back to the keep. Giles returned to Mathilde's side.

"Everything will be fine." Mathilde consoled him. She sighed. "I crave sleep."

"You need meat," he said firmly. "I'll gather a hunting party this day."

"'Tis late, Giles," Mathilde gently chastised him. "Mayhap your men would be better off with their rest this day. Tomorrow is time enough. Go now. I can no longer keep my eyes open."

Vala blinked back tears as she watched a scene that she knew in her heart should be private. Yet Mathilde had insisted that she stay.

Giles reached for Mathilde's hand.

She sucked in a raspy breath. "Take care of the babe."

Mathilde's eyes closed.

Giles released her hand and his eyes sought Vala. "Take care of her. I'll leave early tomorrow morn and return either that day or the next."

"She's weak, Giles," Vala began.

"She's strong," he replied forcefully. "She'll live. You will make it so." He took both her hands. "You are strong. I know this."

"I'll try."

"She'll live," he repeated and drew Vala into a brief hug. "I love you."

And the words had been so rushed that Vala didn't know if she had imagined.

◆

Vala's eyes opened to darkness. Shadows tangled and drifted through the room.

Daughter. The voice trembled.

Vala sat up. A distant baby cried, far away and mournful.

"Nay," she whispered. Not the babe.

A scream lifted through the keep. Vala leapt from her pallet and ran to the bedchamber. The babe lay sleeping, her rosebud mouth pursed. The torch shone on Mathilde, who sat up, a white wraith in the torch lit darkness.

"My babe."

"Asleep safe in her cradle. The babe's cries are trickery."

"The Rogue. You must be strong; he wants you." Mathilde reached for Vala and clasped her hands briefly before letting her go.

"You know?"

"I know many things," Mathilde whispered and reached to gather the fur rug. She offered it to Vala and tucked a corner over herself. "When Edward—that was my husband," Mathilde explained. "When he died, I wanted to die too." Mathilde glanced at Vala from beneath her thick lashes. She was silent for a moment. "I do not know if I can survive this. I hear the babe calling to me."

"You will survive," Vala whispered urgently. "You have a daughter who needs you."

"And a son alone in the afterworld."

"Your husband is there, too." And Vala could have bit her words back if only she could.

"That is why I should be there."

Silence stretched. Even the night sounds within the keep receded into the distance.

"Take my daughter. Name her." Mathilde grasped Vala's hand. "It was meant to be. This is part of the prophecy."

"Nay, Mathilde," Vala said adamantly and sat up, the fur rug pooling around her hips. "Do not speak this nonsense."

"I am so tired, Vala."

Vala chafed Mathilde's cold, limp hand between her own. "You need rest and some healing tonic. Soon you will be yourself."

"It is all right, Vala. I am not scared to die. Much love waits for me," Mathilde said softly. "Take care of Giles. He needs you. He is very much like you."

"He is not like me at all," Vala said softly.

"Soon you will learn how wrong you are," Mathilde replied.

By the next day heavy shadows marred Mathilde's beautiful blue eyes and it was as if the will to live had left her.

The remaining child whimpered weakly through the day as it intermittently sucked on the sugared cloth Vala offered.

Death was close to both mother and child, and Giles was gone. Giles, Vala pressed her thumbs to her temples willing him to hear her. Willing him to come.

"He chooses not to hear," Magna said and stroked her cheek before disappearing.

That night the wind howled around the edges of the keep. The night was black. The moon was almost totally obscured. Vala shivered.

"She will not see another sun set."

Vala swiveled to face Magna.

"Mathilde?"

"Aye."

"There is nothing …?" Vala began.

"Nothing. Her time has come. It has nothing to do with this place or this curse. Her babe needs her."

"As does the babe, she will leave."

"She has you."

A muted light misted the room and warmed the shadows.

"Her soul leaves us," Magna whispered.

"No, Mathilde," Vala cried but the aura around Mathilde was already fading. Peace settled as the soft cries of the dead babe stilled and he was joined with his mother.

Chapter Twenty-nine

"I stayed with her so she was not alone." Vala reached out to him.

Giles jerked away and strode toward the pallet where Mathilde's body lay.

"You knew she was dead. I sent my energy to you and I'm sure Mathilde sent hers."

"I lost Mathilde." He looked at her. "You disliked her from the moment she arrived." He shrugged her away from him and almost threw her off balance. "You did not see fit to tell me that Mathilde was failing?"

"The end came quickly. You were gone much of this day and last. There was no time, Giles." Again she reached for him.

"Did you will her death with your spells and such?"

Vala gasped. "How could you say that?"

"Maybe the Others were not the reason the babes died," he growled. "Maybe Alfred was right."

Vala gasped. "Nay."

These were not words of love nor were they words of a joined destiny. They were words of darkness and despair. And deep within the keep the blackness grew.

◆

Mathilde was buried as the sun rose above the Trees of Truth. The women of Hafne had dug the grave before Giles had arrived with the body. He had fully intended to proceed without them yet he couldn't ask them to leave.

It was a silent group that returned to the keep after the burial. Vala was not among them. He had commanded her absence and already he regretted the command and so many other things. Yet he would not nor couldn't reverse it. He was furious with her, furious that his love had come to this.

Giles glanced around the yard. Editha bustled from the cooking hut. Smoke dulled the sharp morning air as it curled from the new stone building that was the cooking hut. Everywhere people went about their chores but none looked or called to him. It was strangely silent.

Vala had returned to the village. He gazed out onto the hard, dry landscape. Nothing had changed—and yet everything had.

Mathilde was dead and his heart ached for Vala.

Had he been blinded by desire, by need, by Vala? He'd loved Vala and she hadn't returned that love. It was her fault, Vala's, and for all the sense it didn't make, he couldn't help himself. For the first time in his life his attempts at logic failed.

He had failed Mathilde. Vala had failed him. Even the sight had not been there for him in the end. Mathilde had died alone without comfort of those she loved. He had failed his friend Edward. He railed angrily against the fates.

◆

"We'll have to send word of the death," Turstin said at the next day's nooning meal.

Giles grunted. He laid his eating dagger down. The meat was burned and the sauce lumpy. He pushed the food around his trencher. "Editha!" he bellowed. When he stood, the chair slammed backward and the heavy wood toppled to the floor. "Editha!" His roar even silenced the yapping dogs.

"Aye, my lord. You called for me?" Editha stood in the entrance to the hall with her hands on her hips.

"I will not tolerate meals such as these."

"Meals such as what?" Edith asked sweetly. "You do not like it?"

"You know I do not like it. The next meal will be cooked properly."

"As you wish."

Editha marched toward the kitchen before she swung to face him again. "You will regret treating her this way. The Ancients will not tolerate it." She disappeared into the bowels of the keep.

"She is more warrior that woman," Turstin observed.

"As are many here," Giles grumbled. Vala too was a warrior battling for her people and everything she believed in. He had trusted Vala. Worse, he loved Vala. Now a woman he cared for was dead and somewhere on this land was the ever present mewling of the child who had lived.

•

They sat in a circle, knees touching. A gentle hum wrapped like a comfortable cloak around them. Like it had been in the old days, before the troubles, when the land had belonged only to them ... so long ago.

They stared thoughtfully over the still pond.

"I miss it," Magna stated. And they all knew without words that she spoke of the peace that had once been Hafne.

"Won't be long," the one called Zarre assured her.

"Provided the stars align," Mervaine corrected.

"Oh, for the sake of Wodin, speak what you mean. The two must make much of one," Zarre snapped.

Magna smiled and glanced at Mervaine. A complacent smirk rested on his face. Apparently Zarre was oblivious to the fact that his comments were no less obscure than his companions. The way of the Ancients, a way Magna sorely missed. She was ready to go home. She felt a twinge of pain as her thoughts strayed to Vala. Vala would miss her.

•

"She did everything she could to save both Mathilde and her babes," Editha snarled. "I am tired of this feud between both of ye."

Giles admitted to himself that it had been tense the last few days with the women dodging the Normans. Instead he said, "You dare to speak of such?"

Editha shrugged. "This is how you treat her? Without her, neither babe nor mother would have lived. Now one lives."

"She hated Mathilde from the beginning," Giles parried and knew even as he heard the words that they were not true but without anger there was only grief.

"It was the Rogue ere wanted that babe dead. Without Vala his spell would have taken the other babe as well." Editha took in a breath and he knew she was preparing to launch into a fresh tirade. "Remember who saved you when the last drops of your blood were leaking to the keep floor."

This statement sent a thread of guilt racing through Giles. It was true. Vala had saved his life. She had gone into battle again and again. She had been there for him since the beginning. Her hand in his, her body sweetly pressed against his, her … "Enough!"

"And risked her own in the bargain."

He looked at her sharply.

"You and she are not the only ones with the sight." She nodded her head. "It has taken ye long enough to see what is before your very eyes. Just like a man blind to anything that does not involve whoring, food, war or ale. Ye know of what I mean. Ye have seen the third tower. She was there that night and because of ye she faced the Rogue alone and took the second stone."

"I never asked how she got it." Guilt rushed through him and it tasted sour and dry.

"No ye didn't. She went to the third tower alone."

The third tower, it was a place so mystical that it could only be imagined but was their time together nothing more than a dream? "There are many things here, real and imagined," Gile replied.

Editha shook her head. "We are on the edge of war like none you've ever seen."

You exaggerate," Giles replied and knew that she did not. Vala had said the same thing not so many days ago.

"She misses you."

"No."

"You have done her a grave injustice."

He couldn't deny that. His conscience smote him still for that.

"Go to her before tis too late." Editha was nose to nose with him now. "Hafne still needs you. Tell her ye love her."

"Enough, woman," he roared. "You know nothing."

"No?" She smirked at him. "I know your memories return. I know that your mother left you because she had to or you would have died. He would have found you." Editha's face was uncharacteristically dreamy but her words no less cutting. "And you well know it! Your mother never left you! The Ancients took her."

"No!" He shouted and strode away. But there was more anger than confusion.

Had he been hasty? He remembered Vala's tears over Mathilde's pallet. Had she grieved?

Boy, sometimes you surprise even me. Go to her.

Although he couldn't see Magna, he waved her away. He was not ready to deal with her ancient and very annoying bits of wisdom.

Magna appeared before him. "About time you came to your senses, boy."

"Leave!" he commanded.

"Vala's choice decides Hafne's destiny. You are her strength. Go to her."

Magna was again gone.

"Jesu!" He muttered.

Vala needed him. Somehow these were the words able to break the anger and pain of his grief. He had asked Vala to wed first because he needed a wife but last because he loved her. Unfortunately he had failed to tell her, at least not clearly enough for her to understand. And now it was too late, for he would not have what happened to Mathilde, happen to Vala. And he knew his love could do that. There would be no babes and the only way that was possible was to avoid Vala. His love would kill her. He had seen it happen twice before. Women killed because of a man, dying for love, dying after giving birth. He'd seen enough.

You are being ridiculous, Magna droned. *The women of Hafne are stronger than that.*

Was it true? He wondered.

"We are strong for without us there is no Hafne," Adre said over her shoulder as she walked to the well.

Giles rubbed his chin. He did not even know where to look for her. He had not seen Vala since she had moved back to the hut she shared with Magna. She could be anywhere on this land today.

"She is in her hut," Esma said as she bustled by.

Giles started.

"You must hurry." Aedre came up to him. "The evil grows. Her destiny, too, is tied to you."

It was true. He could feel the insidious evil slowly creeping through the keep's walls.

He stormed toward the tiny hut. He pushed the door open without knocking. Inside he was startled to have his path blocked by a goat.

Vala turned and in the dim light she was more beautiful than ever.

"What are you doing here?" she asked.

He needed her. He loved her. He should tell her.

Instead he said, "Return to the keep."

"Just like that," she said. "I think not." She placed the bundle she was holding on the mat by the fire.

He was no good at this. He regrouped and his tongue fumbled with words that would put their destiny back on course. They were words that would convey his feelings to her, words that would make her his, and he hers.

The goat butted and bleated against his hand.

"Pet her and she'll leave you alone."

"By the Apostles, woman, I am not going to pet a goat." The goat continued to ram against him. With a heavy sigh he finally reached down to gingerly touch the top of the goat's head.

"Dara needs milk and tis not safe to leave the goat outside. He does not want another to live."

"Another?" Giles was thrown by the turn of the conversation.

"Another like us. Have you forgotten already. The blood of the three, the bloodline he fears. Have you forgotten the curse, the Rogue, surely not?" She purred. "While you were safe, drinking ale and dicing the evil still roams. Although if I were you I would be more concerned, after all the worst of the evil resides there … with you."

"The stones are united. The parchment says—"

"The parchment says more."

"More?" He stepped farther into the room.

"I can't tell you."

"Why not?"

"I do not know myself." She sighed.

He strode over to the fire and gently peeled the blanket back. The small face looked back at him and for a moment emotion overwhelmed him such as he had never felt before. For it was the image of Mathilde reflected on the tiny, new face. His throat clogged and he turned away as he took a deep breath and fought for control. He took a deep breath and turned around.

"You have called her Dara. A good strong name." Gently he pulled the bit of cloth back over the babe. "I accused you falsely. Mathilde lived for a time because of you."

"Aye, despite that," Vala replied resigned, "I can't return to the keep. Not now, not while the Rogue lives."

"Why?"

"He calls me and I do not know the answer."

"What nonsense do you speak?"

He couldn't help the sudden sadness that came over him nor the fact that she felt it.

"You are saddened. Why?" Concern swept across her beautiful features.

"Nay, frustrated."

"It is Royce who has you saddened."

He swung away from her and long moments passed before he turned back around for he did not want her to see his fear. Fear for her and her safety—for despite his skill as a warrior, this was an enemy he couldn't see and couldn't estimate.

"You miss him," she persisted.

And it was true. But the sorrow of Royce's death and the memories it invoked was something he avoided for it threatened to overwhelm him.

"He took part of my heart when he went." He hesitated before taking a step toward her. "We will not speak of that now."

"As you wish."

"I have missed you." But the words felt thick and unsteady to him and the memories of Royce were too close to the surface.

"Giles," she said softly. "There is not much time."

"We'll speak later."

The hut door shut with a dull thud behind him as if that would end the pain.

But it didn't and it never could.

Chapter Thirty

They appeared before Giles, Magna and two men.

"Jesu! Who are you?"

"We are the Ancients. You remember us as a boy," the most commanding figure of all said as his long white beard trailed in front. "I am Mervaine, but this you know."

"This is nonsense," Giles insisted. "Tis only a dream."

"Cease this foolish talk. There is no more time. Come."

We are as real as you. A voice floated around him.

Overhead the sun settled lower in the sky. The village hum was behind him as he entered the forest. Immediately the trees gathered tight, shutting everything that lay behind.

The pool glittered and just above the placid surface the Ancients glided as if on a sheet of ice. They grouped in the center facing him. Two elders flanked Magna and in the background there were more, but their images were faint.

"Many generations ago you also sprang off an Ancient," Mervaine said.

"Who are you?" Giles demanded.

"Silence!" Mervaine commanded. "The Rogue, I had much hope for him. I sensed his power could one day be more than even mine. It could have done great good."

"There is something that has not been revealed even to me." Magna's scowl clouded her aura. "Always it is about power," she muttered.

"If there was hope, his power couldn't be lost," Mervaine interrupted. "There was no choice."

"You trusted," Magna murmured.

"I shall finish this tale," Mervaine thundered as lightning

cracked and lit the pond. The jagged light skidded and danced over the water.

"There is a verse," Mervaine began. "Long ago written by the gods who created us. I have kept it these many years for it safeguarded Ancient immortality."

"What have you done?" Magna asked.

"I broke trust," Mervaine admitted.

The Grechners who always slept silently deep within the Trees of Truth, awoke with a collective screech. Waves roiled wildly on the pond.

"I did it for the good of Hafne."

"And mayhap for you," Magna persisted.

"Yes, and me. I had chosen him."

"The Rogue," Magna breathed.

"Even after he was banished I couldn't lose all hope." Sadness tinged Mervaine's words. "He blocked what only he knew from me. Even as a child his gift was extraordinary. He was the hope for all the generations of Ancients to come. He would have been one of us, an elder."

Mervaine flung his head back, his arms spread wide. The sky swirled black impenetrable and then shot with violet. Then without warning his eyes met Giles', the intense emerald locking with his and daring him to disbelieve. "I gave him the verse of immortality."

"That is not entirely true," Magna replied. "You should have destroyed the verse instead you hid it and he was able to find it."

"I knew he would. Yet, I couldn't destroy that which he could use. I couldn't give up hope."

"You had faith," Magna replied. "That in itself is not a bad thing.

Mervaine closed his eyes and long eyelashes drifted over pallid cheekbones. "You and Vala. You are what safeguard Hafne. For even then I knew hiding the verse, keeping it, was a mistake." His eyes closed again. "I wanted it so much not to be."

"There is another verse," Mervaine continued. "One even more important than any that has come before. It will save Hafne. His mother awaits its reading. When that is read your work will be done." He was gone in a flash of haze tinged light.

Magna remained. "That is not all. There is more and you know it. Love in three."

"I don't know what you mean?"

"You, and more importantly Vala, must choose."

"This was a dream," he muttered and even as a faint echo bounced from the surrounding rocks it only confirmed what he already knew. This was reality and the magic was real.

•

"Quick my lord," the entire village stood before him as he emerged from the forest.

"Vala is gone," Cyn said.

"What is it? What do you mean she is gone?"

"The Rogue has her. She went to him." Editha frowned.

"Where?" And Giles knew without farther questions.

You must help her choose.

Magna appeared beside him. "You are chosen as is she."

"I know," he said shortly. And anger rose harsh and uninvited within him. He had been a fool. She didn't know what she meant to him. He hadn't told her and now she was in danger. How could he possibly be a husband to her when he couldn't protect her? For that was what he wanted like he had never wanted before, Vala in his bed, his wife, for all the times to come. He sighed heavily. It was too late.

"Do you?" Magna said shortly. "You are special but Vala is so much more. Vala is chosen by him."

"Why?"

"That is what you must answer." She gave him a little push. "Find what Vala needs. It is within both of you."

The smell of onions was almost overpowering. "No matter what you hear, you must stand with her."

"Would I do naught else?" He loved her and he would tell her. After that, he knew naught but he would stand by her.

Magna said nothing.

Magna was right. He had not stood by her after Mathilde's death. Always Vala had been steadfast in her loyalty to the village, to him—to everyone in her life. "I will not disappoint her," he said firmly.

Overhead the Grechners shrieked.

•

From deep in the third tower, Vala watched the Rogue. He muttered charms ignoring her as he had done since he had trapped her hours before. It had been foolishness to come back to this place. But she had ignored the attraction that pulled on her until she could ignore it no longer.

She stood up.

Do not think of it. The words crashed through her conscious so unlike the gentle guidance of Magna. She sat down. The scent of decay was everywhere. A rat scurried over her ankle and she jerked her leg back.

You belong with me.

"Never," she whispered.

He faced her. The face was Wulfgar's, yet not.

"You are mine."

Frost clung to the walls of the tower. Vala shivered.

"Soon you will not feel the cold."

"No."

"By the gods, I created you."

This time the truth of the words was impossible to ignore. There was nowhere to escape. There was only the dreadful cold and those words.

"If I were to come to you," she said in a small voice.

"My love," he purred in a scratchy voice. "I would give you eternal life."

"Happiness?"

"Happiness. What is that? What do you have here? A man who betrays you, another woman's child? Nothing. You have nothing!" His voice rose. "I'll give you everything!"

"It is not true," she desperately whispered.

"Oh, but it is, daughter."

"My father is dead."

"Never!" he roared.

"My father was Norman," Vala persisted, fighting a truth she had known for many days.

"And Ancient."

"Give me proof."

"You were born under the soft light of the early morning moon."

Vala's head jerked up. That was true. "Many babes are."

"Few live." He softly hissed. "Here in Hafne few babes live that are born outside the daylight hours."

She drew back. Magna had told her only days before that she had been born here.

"That is not proof," Vala struggled to keep the quiver from her voice.

"When you were born the knowledge of the ages was in your eyes." He glided closer and tentacles of frost crawled along the floor surrounding Vala. "Like mine."

The frost crystallized and pooled at her feet.

"The truth of your birth was spoken to me only days ago on the clear surface of the pond."

"No."

"Come, daughter." He held out his hand. The wind was gone but the ice still crackled at her feet. His voice rose in a demanding boom that swept through the empty crevices and rotten wood.

Eternal life. The knowledge of the ages.

And the promise was everything and nothing she wanted.

Chapter Thirty-one

"Father," Vala whispered as she struggled to accept the reality she could no longer ignore.

"Vala!" Giles voice was strong and so very close.

"No! Stay away!" Vala screamed.

The Rogue spun. Fetid, cold air swirled around him. "Die!" he roared, rushing forward.

"Nay!" Vala shrieked. She called to every bit of energy in her being. She was devoid of all thought, only one purpose, to save Giles. Her energy shot through the tower. The walls spun gold, trembled and crumbled. The robes of the Rogue lifted and twisted about him. He spun around, disbelieving.

"Daughter?"

"Yes, father!" she shouted over the screech of the wind she had created.

The wind intensified until the being known as the Rogue, her father, banished Ancient, was pinned to the floor by its force. As suddenly, the wind disappeared. Vala collapsed to the floor.

Giles stepped off the ladder and rushed to Vala. He knelt in front of her, his hands cupped her face as he bent and kissed her. The kiss was warm and sweet, and full of promise.

She frowned. "Giles?"

"I thought he had killed you."

"He would never do that," she said dully.

Giles looked deeply into her eyes. "I couldn't bear if anything had happened."

"Leave Giles," Vala replied. "I am tainted."

"Vala." Giles' wrapped his arms around her. "Please. I can't lose you."

Vala twisted away.

"He is not one of us," the Rogue purred.

"He is one of us and so much more. Together, you fear us," Vala replied surprised at the calm in her voice.

"Leave her." Giles stood, legs braced facing an enemy he could never slay. "You only live because Mervaine has allowed it."

"Silence!"

Giles reached down and held his hand out to Vala. "Come with me if you love me."

Vala moved beside him. "No, Giles!" She tugged his arm. "No."

"She is my love. My daughter." The voice was an empty void. The shadowy figure hovered near the top of the tower.

"A few short years with him or eternity with me. Come." The Rogue began to fade.

"No," Vala shouted as Giles' arm drew her against him.

I love you. The voice was soft, laced in tenderness. *You are all I have.*

Vala pushed away from Giles and stood alone facing the Rogue.

"And if I were to come to you?"

"No!"

The voices of the Ancients and Giles wove together.

Vala took a tentative step toward the Rogue and his seductive words.

"I love you, Vala," Giles' voice was strong and sure.

Vala stopped.

Vala, choose Hafne. Choose us. Around the crypt each of the women took the hand of the woman next. All focused their energy to Vala.

"Together we are Hafne's destiny. Together we end the curse. You do not know how much I love you. Without you there is nothing. *Mon amour.* My love." Giles' voice was throaty and oddly sounded choked and his hand was still held out to her.

She should have felt torn. Instead Vala felt the love of the women of Hafne, of the Ancients. The overwhelming faith and trust they placed in her and their destiny and most of all the love that Giles had only just proffered. The choice was no longer difficult. She stepped closer to the Rogue.

The Rogue smiled softly and reached out with pale hands that slipped furtively from beneath his dark robes.

"I do not belong with you. Your soul is already destroyed," Vala sucked in air and reached for the courage that was being offered all around her. "Father or no, I will not go to you."

"You know not of what you speak." His voice was almost a shriek. "You are mine!"

"I am no one's." Vala looked directly at him and her heart pounded. Hafne teetered at this very moment and around her the air was heavy as if everyone and everything held its breath. A tear rolled down her cheek and was followed by another. She loved him like she loved no other. She loved Giles.

"You would whore for the Norman rather than remain with your blood?"

"I would like to forget you are my blood."

"I love you, girl," he said softly.

"You do not. You will not even speak my name."

"Vala."

"It is too late. Except to deny my own existence I wish that you were never my father. I deny you, father!" Vala shouted.

Vala ran.

She left them both behind, the men of her destiny. She stumbled down the fading ladder that led to the third tower. With trembling legs, she jumped to the ground and began to run again. But even as her thoughts went to the pond her feet took her elsewhere.

Editha, Esma and the others called to her. She went to them. There was no choice. Their call overpowered all. She ran without stumbling as the moon lit the darkness, along the treacherous cliff path that led to the cliff, into the unwelcoming darkness of the crypt.

•

"Vala!"

Giles heard the call even while the chill still wrapped around him. The Rogue, weakened from the emotions of the last few minutes, was barely visible on the far side of the tower—and Vala was gone.

Her name echoed through the tower in the voices of the women. The women called to her. The time was ending. She needed him. This was the battle that truly mattered, the battle for her heart and her love.

Father. The word echoed deep in his soul as a mist began to form around the Rogue.

Giles pulled his sword. "I would slay you now."

"If you only could," the Rogue snarled.

"Nay, but someone else will," Giles replied. "She has waited for many centuries for that honor."

Giles hurried down the ladder as the women of Hafne called his name.

•

The crypt was alive with the energy of those seen and unseen. The power of the combined will of so many souls was intoxicating. Giles staggered. He reached for Vala.

"No, Giles," she said and walked toward the crypt, toward the women.

"Vala, wait. I love you," Giles persisted.

A crack appeared in the rock overhead and faint light showed.

"It does not matter. I am tainted," Vala replied and regret made her stomach clench. She was not this strong, not strong enough to walk away yet for his sake she had to be. Love couldn't overcome the truth of who she was.

"You, too, are Ancient, Norman, Saxon. As am I," Giles reminded her. "Hafne needs us."

The Ancients whispered, comforting sounds that swirled around them.

"He is here. I am never rid of his shadow." Vala kept walking as if that would stop the grief. She wiped a hand across her eyes. They were hot, dry and empty, like her soul as the grief bit deep.

Daughter—but the call was desperate, faint. A black shadow reached across the rock outcropping. Ice formed as the temperature dived.

Vala quivered.

The ancient elders materialized one after the other. They stood in a line again, as always, Magna flanked by the men.

"I am tired child," Magna said. "Release me. Break the curse."

Vala shook her head. "Don't go. I love you," she muttered softly.

"I love you too, child. That is why you will let me go."

"Let her go?" Giles breathed beside her. "What do you mean?"

Suddenly Magna stood beside Giles. He could feel her presence faint but there. The smooth skin of young hands touched his wrist. "My work is almost done, go to her."

And he did, with his hands on her shoulders Giles turned her to face him. His words were so soft they were a mere caress meant for her ears only. "Sweet Vala I would die without you by my side. I love you like no other. Even without your love I want you here with me."

She shuddered and looked into his dear face, so strong yet so vulnerable. "You have told me many times this day and I have not believed."

"I love you. I would die for you."

"And almost did." She tentatively touched his cheek. "I couldn't love any man more."

"Ah, Vala. We are destined and he that is your father. His destiny is so very different from ours."

"What are you saying, Giles.?

"I'm not sure. I only know what Mervaine has told me."

She stepped back frowning. "Told you? Mervaine."

"Aye. It is impossible to not believe in magic when faced with him. I would not want to meet him in battle." He pulled her so tightly to him that for a minute her breath left her. "Do not leave me. I am nothing without you."

"Release me," she murmured and not only did he let her go but he turned her around to face the one task that was left. She stood, facing what might have been her destiny with the strength of Giles' hands on her shoulders and the courage of Hafne behind her.

"Father, quit this place. 'Tis over." There was new strength in Vala's voice.

"My own child, you would destroy me rather than join me?"

"You should never have lived."

"Then neither would you."

"But you did and I do. It is over now. The misery of the people, the killing must end. I have found love. The curse will be broken."

She sucked in a deep breath as those around her only waited. "Father I refute you," Vala said and stepped so close to him that the icy air seemed to slice through her skin.

"No!"

"Father, I love the Norman. I choose him. It is over."

"You can't." The words were distant as the darkness began to lift.

"I love Giles," she said before turning to Giles. "Only you, always."

"And I love you." Giles took her hands holding them tight.

Love is nothing, the voice of the Rogue roared in a broken chipped voice.

Love. Have they both spoken of love? Mervaine's deep voice floated overhead. Magna held her staff and leaned against the shoulder of Mervaine. This time the words floated around them as if carried by fairies on the breeze.

Love.

The words were softly enunciated in a woman's cultured voice. Rock cracked overhead and dropped around them. Moonlight filtered brightly down.

A bolt of lightning lit the entire crypt.

Voices whispered on all sides. Still it was not over as the temperature plunged once again.

Mervaine waved his staff in the air and light flashed purple and orange against the rock. "Speak! Justice will be done this day!"

Overhead a woman emerged faint in the mist as she fluttered overhead. "My son. I have waited a long time for this."

The Rogue's voice cracked with effort. "I killed you years ago. Why can't you die?"

"Oh, I will my son, I will. But I'll take you with me."

"You can't. I am immortal and I am no one's son."

"Neither tis true, my son."

"Did you not hear the verse Mervaine left?" The Rogue snarled.

"I did. But there is more that you do not know."

"Nay."

"I have carried the words with me all these years." She hovered beside him the look on her face gentle. "Why did you have to do it? You could have been so much. I loved you once."

Her gentle voice filled the crypt but it was only the end of the verse that echoed in Vala's memory for that was all that mattered.

Should the spawn of your blood deny your truth
Death will be theirs

The Rogue seemed to weaken visibly, his image fading as if the verse had taken what strength he had.

"Daughter!" He cried weakly.

Vala pinched her eyes shut and clutched Giles' hand. "This is of what you spoke."

"Aye." He squeezed her hand and whispered, "I love you, always."

"She denies you," the ghost that was the Rogue's mother said. "Come." She held her arms out to him. "It is your time."

"No." But the Rogue's voice was weak as the verse of a long forgotten god ended the life he had found. Both entities, mother and son, faded and disappeared from the crypt.

"Is he gone?" Vala whispered. "I want never to see him again father or no."

"He is gone, but it is not over. Not yet," Magna said. "Gather the women."

"We must read the parchment. These dribs and dabbles are not good enough, we know the end but naught else." Editha pointed to Esma and Aedre. "Bring your pieces forward."

"How did you find it?" Vala asked.

"Magna gave them to me for safekeeping. For it is not just you, all of us are responsible for Hafne," Editha replied.

The parchment that they had returned whole to the cliff beneath the Tree of Truth was again in three, returned to the crypt and in the hands of Editha, Aedre and Esma. Each ragged edge began to glow as if still being held to the fire that had original torn it.

"It is the fire of the Rogue's inception," Vala said, as the words and the truth seemed to come from nowhere. "It holds the memory of that day."

Giles was silent. The truth was in the hum of the paper. He glanced at Vala. Her face was white as was each of the women whose faces glowed in the torchlight. Fire had breathed the beginning of what now befell this land. Fire would end it. The hum ceased.

The parchment was whole. The Ancients began to chant softly as the people of Hafne gathered around. Editha read the words they had long waited to hear.

Peace when
the one Yane has spawned

Denies him
the one Yane destroyed
Takes him
The love of three; Saxon, Ancient, Norman.
Returns the stone

"He was named," Vala breathed.

"Yes," Editha replied. "He was named and now we may use his name. In the stories we'll tell our children and they will tell their children. They must know so they will be prepared, should it ever happen again."

"It will not," Esma said confidently.

The manuscript fell from Editha's hands and shattered into shards. The pieces skittered across the ground, blown by a breeze that seemed to rise from still air, and disappeared into emptiness.

Chapter Thirty-two

For the second time in as many days Giles and Vala stood before the pond but this time Vala carried the babe, Dara. The moon's full light bathed the clearing. The time had finally arrived.

The Ancients gathered at the forefront, the women of Hafne beside, and the Saxon men and the Normans flanked the rear. The Trees of Truth shone lime green and their leaves reflected off the still pond.

Mervaine slowly skimmed the pond's still surface. One Grechner sat, as he had those many centuries before, perched on Mervaine's shoulder.

The hum gained in strength as the Ancient elders, Mervaine, Magna and Zarre, chanted in transparent unison over the still water of the pond. The pond slowly came alive as the waves rocked the surface.

"Speak up, girl!" Mervaine roared.

"I love the Norman!" Vala said clearly. "I love you, Giles."
Giles wrapped his arms around her and the babe, Dara. "I love you, too," he said thickly. "Both of you."

The women of Hafne gathered around Vala, Giles and the babe. Overhead the Grechners screeched and a hum filled the air as the Trees of Truth sang.

Mervaine held his hands wide. "Come to me child."

Vala passed the babe to Giles and walked toward the light and power that was Mervaine.

"You are one of us, part of the Ancients. That blood runs strongly through you, stronger than anything else. Stronger than any others." He glanced to Giles before returning his attention to Vala. "Do not forget your father for he was what we all have the ability to become." He touched her lightly on the head. Warmth flooded her body. "Remember, you are as much one of us."

He motioned to the women of Hafne with a wave of his hand. "As you all are, Saxon, Norman, and those of the three. You are Hafne."

Azure sparks danced from his staff. "The stones," he commanded.

Vala and Giles carried the stones toward Mervaine who floated just above the surface of the pond.

"As it was foretold," Mervaine boomed. The stones lay quietly in the palms of his hands, held wide to the heavens. "So they shall return. The people of Hafne joined under one sky, the love of three, the parchment three—read and," he looked seriously at Vala. "The true choice made, the right choice, the choice of love." His attention returned to the open skies above him.

"Mend the seers' stone, break the curse, restore peace to Hafne. Serpent to dust, rot to love, peace to Hafne!"

Thunder cracked, the stones rose, shot purple across the pond, and reflected on every face gathered around the water, every face in Hafne. Then they joined together with a bang that shuddered through the Trees of Truth and silenced the screeches of the Grechner. Then the stones dropped quickly and silently into the pond.

"It is over for now," Mervaine said. And then he was gone.

◆

But it was not over.

Vala knew worse was still ahead of her. Her gut twisted in anticipation of that sorrow. Still, she walked toward the keep with Hafne's women beside her. She had promised Magna she would let her go.

You do not need me.

"I'll always need you," Vala choked out.

"As do we all," Esma replied. "Magna, show yourself."

Three towers stood clear. The women surrounded Vala, each reaching for another's hand. Flames exploded into the early predawn sky. Through a cloud of fire, Magna hovered over the third tower. Her iron gray hair twisted around her head as she waved her staff furiously around her and she invoked an incantation.

Beneath her, the third tower collapsed.

"Magna, no!" Vala screamed and realized before the words flew from her mouth that they were futile. She would have run to Magna but for the babe in her arms. The babe began to wail even as tears threatened to spill from Vala's eyes.

Goodbye, child.

"No," Vala whispered in a broken voice. "I can't lose you, never you." But the prophecy was fulfilled. Magna was not needed.

A warm breeze whispered around her in a gentle caress.

Tis as it was written.

Strong arms wrapped around her and she leaned against Giles. He was warm and solid, and his energy enfolded her more tightly than even his arms ever could.

"Peace at last." Editha's voice broke the moment and behind her the villagers erupted in cheers. The scent of onions mixed with roses and wafted lightly around them.

Do not let him go girl.

"I know, Magna, he is ..." Her words broke off as she glanced up at Giles and smiled crookedly at him.

"The One," they said in unison with the babe pressed between them.

•••

Ryshia Kennie

"In the inevitable search for love, there are many land mines but dodging them is half the fun and that's the secret of my stories," says Canadian author, Ryshia Kennie. In her travels there have been many unexpected and amazing things, and the memories of those are only the beginning of her fictional adventures. From earthquakes in Hawaii to being chased by enraged water carriers in Morocco to deep sea fishing trip gone slightly askew in Venezuela—it all happened.

Ryshia's first Black Lyon release, FROM THE DUST, is the touching story of man and woman in a time of toil and desperation during the summer of 1935 in the Qu'Appelle District, Saskatchewan. Her writing takes a different, fantastical turn in the story you've just read: RING OF DESIRE. To learn more about Ryshia visit:

www.RyshiaKennie.com
www.Ryshia.Blogspot.com

RYSHIA KENNIE

Love can be so... unexpected.

In the spring of 1935, understated beauty Eva Edwards is widowed. A blessing to be sure. Having long since left England, a rare talent for music and notions of love behind, her one focus is keeping her farm and raising a child not her own—no matter the sacrifice and struggle.

Born of wealth, veterinarian Tate Prescott Brown has come to the dust of Saskatchewan's rural Qu'Appelle District to find independence and take possession of his farm—Eva's farm. Now, in an effort to solve a legal misunderstanding, Tate faces a sacrifice and struggle of his own: to do what he thinks is right by Eva ... or what's right for his heart.

ISBN: 978-0-9793252-6-7
Price: $16.95 paperback

"A solid romance that also has a good deal to offer to those who don't normally read romances." –Dan W. Hays, The Statesman Journal

"The plot was so well written, and the people so endearing that it was impossible to not love this book." –The Romance Studio

"A perfect blend of history and romance." –M. Jean Pike, Author

"A wonderful setting, good, strong characters and a romance to take your breath away." –Simply Romance Reviews